# FLAT WHITE LIES

# by A.A. Abbott

Published by Perfect City Press.

This book was written by a British writer in British English.

**PAPERBACK EDITION**

**ISBN 978-1-913395-11-7**

# A FEW WORDS OF THANKS

Thanks to my editor, Katharine D'Souza, and everyone else who helped make this book great, especially Ali AElsey, Andrea Neal, Andrew Maxwell, Callie Hill, Colin Ward, David Wake, David Ward, Dawn Abigail, Dawn Bolton, Donna Morfett, Elizabeth Hill, Gaye Davis, Graham Whitwell, Helen Combe, Helen Shepherd, Lucienne Boyce, Jeremy White, Jill Griffin, Jo Ullah, John Lynch, Katherine Evans, Lesley Lloyd, Lucy Gage, Margaret Egrot, Michèle Weibel, Michelle Armitage, Nicki Collins, Nigel Howl, Punam Farmah, Suzanne H Ferris, Suzanne McConaghy, Tom Blenkinsop, Tom Bryson and Zoe Thompson.

**A.A. Abbott**
England, August 2023

# Contents

# CHAPTER 1

## JENNA

I saw them peer through the window, blocking Bristol's autumn sunshine with their bulk. While it was pleasantly warm in my cafe, I shivered, already on edge. I'd just received emails hiking my car insurance and increasing the rent. How could I afford it?

The pair of burly men unsettled me further. Like giant crows circling, they hovered outside. It triggered memories of the cops coming round after my mother's death. That had been almost a decade ago, though. Why would they return now? Anyway, these guys wore black bomber jackets rather than police uniform.

"Are you okay?" Andrew looked up from his laptop.

"Grit in my eye," I lied, rubbing at one of them. "You ordered a flat white, didn't you?"

"With an extra shot. How else do you kick-start Monday?"

One of the men outside began speaking on his phone. They both moved out of sight. I exhaled, relaxing into the café's cosy atmosphere. Scents of butter, sugar and spice lingered in the air. Pink paint and candy-striped bunting added to the sweetness. They'd been a labour of love, my personal stamp on the premises when I'd opened as Jenna's Cupcakery. Most days, I matched the retro feel with fifties-inspired clothing. This morning, I'd thrown on a full-skirted flowery dress, ballet flats, and thick make-up. A carnival glass choker glittered at my neck. It threw rainbow flashes onto the walls when it caught the light.

This was almost the future I'd mapped out with Mum. We both enjoyed baking. I'd always adored a vintage vibe, too. When I grew up, she said, we'd open a coffee bar together, converting the front room of our family B&B in Minehead. I would fill it with cute knick-knacks, cakes and smiling customers.

I thought it would never happen after she died, but at last, I'd transplanted my dream to Bristol. Here in Clifton, a suburb of my adopted city, I made cakes to die for. The only problem was money. Costs had risen so much that my business was struggling to survive.

Customers like Andrew, friendly and appreciative, helped me forget my stress. After four visits, I considered him a regular. I selected a plain white cup for him. Floral designs dominated our collection of mismatched crockery, but he might not thank me for choosing one. A rich aroma rose from the espresso machine. Its clatter drowned out both the Coldplay soundtrack and the tapping of Andrew's fingers on his laptop.

I risked a glance at him. He'd taken the table nearest the counter, close enough to see the concentration in his grey eyes. Warmth flooded through me as I observed his soft tawny curls, freshly trimmed beard and tanned skin. His charcoal wool blazer and cream shirt were smarter than his usual gear. He must have a meeting later.

I'd sworn off men after splitting with Ned, but perhaps I could make an exception for Andrew. My mind drifted to a place where he would take me in his arms. His tall frame towering above me, he would stroke my long black hair and cuddle my cares away.

It was a crazy fantasy, worthy of an adolescent rather than a twenty-six-year-old business owner. When Andrew caught my eye, I reddened. Fortunately, my thick Pan Stik masked the blushes. I hoped he wouldn't guess my thoughts either.

"I'll take a cinnamon cupcake with it, please," he said.

Sam, my sole employee, broke off from chatting to our only other customer. I didn't recognise her. A forty-something with a sleek ponytail, she wore a Lycra vest and leggings under her trench coat. The gym gear contrasted with a full face of make-up.

If she was trying too hard with her appearance, Sam had made no effort at all. He looked as if he'd just tumbled out of bed and stopped at a charity shop to buy jeans on his way to work. "The cinnamon is a good choice. I had one for breakfast," he told Andrew.

"You've sampled all the cakes, then?" Andrew asked.

Sam smacked his lips. "It would be rude not to."

"But you're thin as a rake." The gymgoer scanned his tight jeans and T-shirt, her gaze predatory. She plainly admired waifish types with messy blond man-buns. I preferred Andrew's more grown-up style.

Sam didn't seem to mind being sized up like a piece of meat. "I don't eat anything else," he told her.

It might be true. I couldn't afford to pay more than the minimum wage, and that didn't go far in Bristol. Luckily for Sam, his girlfriend earned good money. He wouldn't be living in trendy Montpelier otherwise.

"Maybe I should try one too," the woman said.

"It's lush with a cappuccino," Sam suggested. "Jenna can make you a skinny one, with a dusting of chocolate. How's that?"

"Sounds gert lush, as you Bristolians put it."

Sam didn't point out we both came from Minehead, further down the coast. "Where are you from?" he asked.

"London."

Andrew butted in. "A refugee from the capital? My estate agent friends say they've seen an influx. Clifton is much sought after, especially this area. They call it the village."

"I fell in love with it when I lived here as a student," I admitted.

Andrew nodded. "It's the best part of Bristol, with prices to match."

He wasn't wrong. Since I'd bought my flat five years earlier, its value had spiralled. The rent I paid for the café was insane, though.

"Clifton doubles up for London in films," Sam said. "We shot my last one in an old Georgian square around the corner. It stood in for Mayfair."

"You make films?" The woman's face twitched, astonishment obviously battling Botox.

"I'm an actor. Paid to fake it. I had a supporting role that time, but it was great experience."

I stifled a giggle. Sam had lamented that he didn't even get to speak in the movie, a drama about supermodels. He'd painstakingly learned his lines, only for the director to cut them from the script.

"So why are you here?" she asked.

"Resting, my love." Sam was used to the question. Customers often recognised him from an obscure art house film or a bit-part on Netflix. Over and over, I'd heard him explain that acting didn't pay the bills, and wasn't he lucky to work for his best friend?

Before the blonde quizzed him further, though, he asked, "And what brings you to our cupcakery on this fine September morning?"

"A pitstop. I'm on my way back from an aerobics class."

"Back to where? Not London, surely?" Sam raised an eyebrow.

I was happy for him to flirt if it made her drop in again. With my overdraft knocking on its limit and credit cards maxed out, we desperately needed more business.

Her reply oozed smugness. "Actually, I've swapped a dinky studio in Stratford for a lovely cottage here. Roses round the door, the works. My boss doesn't care where I am, as long as the job gets done." She added, "I'm a journalist."

Sam's eyes shone like a kid at Christmas. "Well, I hope you'll write good things about us."

"I would if I could, but I'm afraid I produce features for engineering journals. Boring. It means I can work at home and sample all of Clifton's fine coffee shops, though. You're my tenth."

"That's my lucky number," Sam said. "Do come back and make Jenna's Cupcakery your coffee bar of choice. You can rely on me to look after you."

"I'm sure I can." She fluttered false lashes at him, clearly hungry for more than cake.

I was grateful when Andrew rescued Sam by rejoining the conversation. "Didn't I see you at the Nuffield gym last week?" he asked her. "Crushing it on the cross trainer, I thought."

She preened, flicking her ponytail. "Yes, are you a member there too?"

"I had a trial, but joined an online class instead." Andrew pointed to the door. "Hey, your baking has attracted fans, Jenna."

Coldplay's ballad faded, replaced by the sound of blood pounding through my ears. The grim duo had returned.

As the door opened, the café suddenly seemed small and dark. The two men filled the space, black clothes sucking up the light. Their faces were pale, podgy, and bleak. These guys didn't look like Bake-Off groupies.

I finished making Andrew's flat white, omitting the usual flourish of a heart in the foam. My hands were shaking too much for barista art.

"Good morning, gents, can I interest you in our special offer? Buy a cupcake and get any regular size hot drink for a pound." Sam didn't miss a chance to run his patter.

"Will I be getting my cappuccino for a pound too?" his new friend demanded.

"Of course you will, my love."

The men marched up to the counter, ignoring Sam. One of them was obviously in charge, his companion deferring to him as he spoke. "Miss Jenna Wyatt?" he asked, in a growly local accent.

"That's me." I smiled, trying to hide my nerves. "I'll be with you as soon as I've served this gentleman."

Andrew stood up. "Let me help, Jenna. Here, hand me the coffee."

10

I gave him the cup and saucer. "And a cinnamon cupcake too, isn't it?" I lifted the dome covering the flowery porcelain cake stand. A blast of spice caught my nostrils.

"That one, please." Andrew pointed. "Bring on the bling."

I'd sprinkled the swirls of creamy icing with gold dragées. Andrew wanted the glitziest example. In different circumstances, I'd have chuckled at his fancy choice. I couldn't manage a smile right now, though. It was a win when I plated up the cake without dropping it.

"Thanks," Andrew said, placing the refreshments next to his laptop. He sat down to work again.

"So, how can I help?" I asked.

"Miss Wyatt," the first man said. "We're bailiffs, appointed by the court over a debt you owe to a Mr Edward Cramer in the sum of sixty-two thousand, three hundred and seventy-five pounds."

"Ned?" My head was spinning. I gripped the counter. Once I'd steadied myself, I gasped, "I owe him how much?"

He repeated the amount, unzipping a document case and showing me an official-looking writ. "If you want to satisfy yourself about my identity, you're welcome to phone my office," he said. "This is me. Steve Evans." He showed me the ID card attached to a lanyard around his neck.

His colleague did the same. He was Lee Murraymore.

"Can you make an immediate payment?" Evans asked.

It would be easier to fly to the moon. I stared at him.

"Wait." Sam slipped across to stand beside them. He was a head shorter, dwarfed by the newcomers, but his change in tone commanded their attention. "Where's your evidence she owes this money?"

"We have a writ," Evans said. "You've heard of a county court judgement?"

"Mind if I see?" Sam inspected it. "Jenna, did you know you had a CCJ? How did it happen?"

My words tumbled out in short, breathy bursts. "It started when Ned moved out," I said. In truth, the problem had begun before then, but I lacked the energy to explain. "He told me I owed him money and he'd make sure to collect it."

Sniffing, I recalled the pile of unopened post on my kitchen table. If the court had sent an envelope with red writing, it would have ended up there.

Evans' face remained impassive. "I asked if you can pay the full amount, Miss Wyatt. If you're unable to, we'll have to seize goods—"

"You can't take anything from the café," Sam protested. "These are the tools of her trade."

"We're talking to Miss Wyatt, if you don't mind," Evans said.

"So am I. If you don't mind." Sam turned to me. "I've met their sort before. Don't give them anything. Without the fixtures and furniture here, you can't run your business. Trust me on this, Jenna." Despite a baleful glance from Andrew, he reached for my hand and gripped it.

I squeezed back. Knowing Sam's family, I suspected they had bailiffs round regularly.

"Can you take us round to your flat, please, Miss Wyatt?" Evans said. His approach seemed matter of fact, as if he was asking me for a cake recipe. "You see, we know it's not far. And that's your car parked outside, isn't it? It would save a lot of trouble if you'd hand over the keys to Lee so we don't have to clamp it."

"Ignore him," Sam advised. "You need the car for your business. Without it, you can't get supplies. You're under no obligation to let him into your flat so he can start stripping it."

Evans lost patience. "I'm sorry, Miss Wyatt, but you're being misinformed. If you can't pay, we will remove goods and sell them to raise funds to apply towards the sum outstanding."

Andrew knocked back his coffee and powered down his laptop. "Must go. Meetings wait for no man." His expression exuded sympathy as he held out a credit card. "Take care, Jenna. I'll see you soon, all right?"

The gym bunny gave Sam a tight smile. "Got to dash too. Can I settle up, please?"

"Pleasure, my love." He took payment from her phone.

I doubted we'd see her again. It would be a miracle if Andrew returned either. A pang of regret added itself to my tension.

"You're wasting your time," Sam said to Evans. "I think you should leave."

"I'm only doing my job," Evans said. "I appreciate the situation isn't easy for Miss Wyatt, but nor is it pleasant for Mr Cramer. He is owed a substantial amount."

I saw only one way out of the stalemate. Much as I hated it, I had to talk to my ex-fiancé. He'd caused all this trouble. "I'll ring Ned."

"Right," Sam said. He glared at the men in black.

Murraymore's forehead wrinkled. "Shouldn't we—"

Evans didn't let him finish. "Let's see," the senior bailiff said.

I picked up my phone, breath quickening as I tapped my ex's number. Even the memory of his voice resulted in a surge of desire. Our break-up hadn't been my choice, and although he'd cheated on me, I'd have taken him back if he'd asked.

"Jenna?"

I shrank at the unexpected note of triumph in his voice.

"You sent bailiffs," I stammered.

"And?"

"They say I owe you sixty thousand pounds. It's unbelievable. I mean, I know you helped me set up the café and I'd have to pay you back eventually, but how come it's so much?"

'He stayed with you rent-free,' Sam mouthed.

"You lived in my flat for free. I cooked for you, ironed your shirts, and—"

Sam paled, perhaps afraid I'd supply too much information.

"—we were in a relationship." I began to sob.

"The key word is 'were'. It's done with. Over. You signed loan documents and I want my money back. The court agrees you have to pay. Simple as that."

"I can't possibly afford it." I trembled, the phone almost slipping from my hand.

Sam put an arm around my shoulder and guided me to the seat furthest away from Evans.

"Jenna? Jenna." Ned's tone softened to a wheedle. "There's an easy way to solve this. Transfer your flat to me in satisfaction of the debt. You won't even have to pay the mortgage. I'll take it on too. Listen, I've got my lawyers onside, ready to go. I can send you the paperwork this afternoon."

My body tensed. He'd taken a step too far. "I can't believe you're serious," I said. "Even after the mortgage, my equity in the flat is worth more than sixty thousand pounds."

"Really?" Ned's public school vowels dripped with sarcasm.

I used to find his voice sexy, but not now. "Yes, really," I said. "So you work for a merchant bank in London, and you're a financial expert, but I know what my own property is worth."

"Evidently you don't. Face facts, Jenna. It's a fire sale. You need money quickly, and you haven't got it, have you?"

I pictured his smirk. At that moment, I hated him. How stupid did he think I was?

"Just tell him no," Sam whispered.

"No. You're out of order, Ned." Heat rose to my cheeks. I swallowed, wishing I'd opened those letters before it was too late.

Ned turned off the charm like a tap. "Fine," he snapped. "I want that cash in my bank account by Friday."

"That's unreasonable," Sam snatched the phone. His Somerset burr was gone. "Miss Wyatt needs two weeks from today. She will make the payment in full."

"Who is this?" Ned demanded, tinny voice still loud enough to hear.

"Her lawyer," Sam lied. He sounded the part. The Royal Family would have been proud of him.

Evans nudged his colleague. He stared at Sam with amusement.

"I find it hard to believe Jenna can raise sixty grand just like that. How's she going to do it?" Ned's sneer was audible.

"It's none of your business how she does it. Just tell your Rottweilers to leave her premises."

Evans didn't seem offended. His craggy features quivered, as if suppressing a laugh. Meanwhile, Ned could be heard sighing and saying he supposed he could give it a fortnight.

"So that's agreed, then. I don't think there's any more to say, is there?" Sam cut the call. He jerked a thumb at the door. "Out."

Murraymore grunted.

"Just a moment, Sir," Evans said. "As we've been appointed by the court to collect the debt, I need to check with my office that a two-week payment deadline is acceptable to the creditor."

"But you heard him say so," Sam protested.

"Even so, I'm obliged to make sure."

Murraymore stared longingly at the coffee machine while his boss phoned their support team. Whoever Evans spoke to, they were more discreet than Ned. I couldn't hear a word from them as Evans explained the situation.

Sam busied himself clearing crockery and wiping down tables. I slumped into the seat vacated by Andrew, too drained to move. Sam had done his best for me, but he'd only shunted my problems a short while into the future. I couldn't raise sixty thousand pounds today, and I had no idea how to do it in a fortnight either. I felt sick.

Eventually, Evans finished his conversation. "Good news, Miss Wyatt. It's agreed, so we'll be on our way. Goodbye."

He strode outside, Murraymore shuffling after him. The door slammed shut.

"I was wrong," Sam said. "They're not Rottweilers, just gorillas. Morons. And that ex of yours is the biggest dick I've ever met. I knew it the moment I laid eyes on him."

My breath stilled for a heartbeat. "You never said."

Sam hesitated. "I didn't want to lose you as a friend. But why do you always fall for that type? Searching for a father figure, I suppose."

"Father figure? Ned was only five years older than me."

"And he behaved like it was fifty. Boasting about his amazingly important job, knocking back wine and treating you like a slave. Who else might have done that? Your deadbeat stepfather, for instance? And look how Ned used you."

"This is getting us nowhere." Flopping forward in my chair, head in my hands, I twisted a lock of hair around my fingers. I pulled it tight until my scalp hurt. "How can I find that kind of money in fourteen days?"

# CHAPTER 2

## JENNA

Sam locked the door and set the sign on it to CLOSED. "You'll do it," he said, "but on your terms, not Ned's. First, you need caffeine. How about I make you coffee?"

"Yes, please."

"And would madam like a cupcake with that?"

"I can't face food."

Still, my nausea eased as he pressed buttons on the machine, producing a cappuccino and adding a smiley emoji with the cocoa shaker.

"Here," he presented it with a flourish, "Vincent's finest."

"Vincent's Coffee is the very best." I parroted the pink and gold placard which nestled among the dishes of cakes on the counter.

It was another homage to Mum. She'd always served Vincent's Coffee at the B&B, and customers adored it. Mum praised it as a luxury brand, the best, and no less than our guests warranted. When they chose us for their holidays, they could expect to be pampered.

Memories flooded in, of Mum frying bacon and brewing coffee while I took the part of waitress in a black dress she'd bought at Marks & Spencer. I must have been no more than ten years old when I started, young enough that I was often complimented for assisting in the family business. After working every morning, our afternoons were free. Mum and I usually went to the beach. It seemed the sun always shone, but of course, it would during the summer.

Looking back, I wasn't sure how she coped during term times. I would have been away at boarding school. The B&B was less busy then, and perhaps Richard helped. She'd fallen out with her family and didn't have relatives to lend a hand. More likely, she managed without Richard or anyone else. He certainly made himself scarce when I was around. I merely had hazy recollections of him, at least until the day she died.

Richard had spotted the cops through the window and hissed at me to say he wasn't in. I'd guessed he'd committed a minor misdemeanour while under the influence. It wasn't unknown. Yet, when they established who I was and told me they had bad news, I'd said, "You'd better talk to Dad."

I was seventeen, and still thought Richard was my father. No-one had yet said otherwise. Mum had married him before I was born; she'd put his name on my birth certificate. When I fetched him, the police had explained there had been a pile-up on the M5 motorway. A sudden gust of smoke from harvest fires had made it impossible for drivers to see. The traffic moved so fast that a crash was inevitable. Mum had died on impact, the truck behind her old Renault shoving it into the lorry in front.

That was the end of my childhood, and the beginning of the end of my relationship with Richard.

Grief made him withdraw into himself. He did even less work than before, visiting pubs more often. My presence was a necessary evil, required for cleaning and tidying and making breakfasts. Richard announced I'd be leaving boarding school because he couldn't afford the fees anymore. While that may have been true, the real reason was that he needed me to take over Mum's toil.

At least I'd fitted in a final year of A Level studies at the local college. Richard had grudgingly agreed to it, provided the guests stayed happy. The pace had been relentless, but I'd pulled it off.

Moisture filled my eyes. I'd tried so hard to please him in that year before my eighteenth birthday, and then he'd broken the news. I was not his child: I was an adult now, and as he no longer had responsibilities towards me, he was selling up and moving to Turkey.

Richard didn't waste his time after that. He wouldn't tell me who my real father was. In all likelihood, he had no idea. The next day, a sale sign hung outside the B&B; within a week, he'd agreed terms with a buyer.

As far as I knew, he was still sunning himself, enjoying retirement. Once I started university in Bristol, I didn't hear from him again. He'd got a good price for the B&B, but he'd probably drunk it all since. None of the proceeds came to me. Richard and Mum had owned the property together, so her share went to him on her death. He'd offered me nothing then, and it was unlikely he'd help me now. Even if I tracked him down, even if he'd invested the money sensibly, I doubted he'd give me a penny.

Tears fell as I scolded myself for giving space in my head to Richard. He wasn't worth it, and nor was Ned. I made an effort to bring my thoughts back to my mother, sniffing the strong aroma of Vincent's coffee in the cup set before me. A droplet splashed into it.

"Hey," Sam said. "Don't dilute it, drink it." He perched opposite me, crossing his legs. With his delicate features and slight build, he reminded me of a pixie.

I took a sip, savouring the rich taste. "It will break my heart to close the café," I said. "but I don't know how much longer it can survive. Our bills are rising through the roof, and we don't get enough trade to cover them. And now this."

"We'll get through it."

I sniffed, so grateful for his friendship that it was almost too much to bear. I'd never be able to talk to another employee like this. "I'm so sorry," I said. "I forgot it's not just my livelihood on the line, but yours. Your job will go too."

"Don't worry about me," Sam said. "I might land a big role tomorrow. And if I don't, I'll find something else. But it won't come to that."

"How can you be so sure? Even if you're right, and the bailiffs can't grab the furniture—"

He nodded. "I am. Take it from me."

"—I can't pay. As well as the business, I'll lose my flat, because it's the only valuable asset I've got. Ned will get his hands on it, or he'll force me to sell it. I just don't know what to do." It would hurt nearly as much as letting the café go under. Clifton was my favourite part of the city. My apartment, a few minutes' walk away, sat at the top of a tall Georgian townhouse. I had a view of the tree-lined Avon Gorge, with Brunel's suspension bridge soaring dramatically above. It was my haven.

"There's always a way," Sam said. "Remember? I was resigned to a life in sales when you insisted I applied to theatre school."

I lifted my chin slowly, as if it held a lead weight. "Sales? You mean market trading. Anyway, that was then. We were only sixth formers. I thought I knew everything, but the opposite was true."

"All the same, you were right. Acting was just my dream, but you encouraged me to follow it. Let me support you to follow yours," Sam said softly. He gestured around the room. "You love this, don't you – the vintage feel, the Vincent's coffee, the cupcakes? We'll get that cash to him somehow."

I hyperventilated, misgivings increasing by the minute. "You're not robbing a bank," I gulped.

"Whoa. Not quite what I had in mind." Sam leaned back. "You can remortgage to pay Ned off. I've got contacts."

"Loan sharks? No chance." My breath still emerged in short, sharp bursts.

"Funny you mention that. I've got a cousin in the trade, but you don't want to be tangling with him. He's the kind of guy who makes Steve Evans look like the Pope. No, I meant my brother Ryan's fiancée. She's a mortgage broker."

"That would be Ryan who was arrested last month for receiving stolen goods?" I asked, folding my arms, fingernails digging into my biceps.

Sam shrugged. "Everyone makes mistakes."

# CHAPTER 3

## A MAN WITH A PROBLEM

The phone call came at the worst possible time. He and Sheila had just finished dinner in the red room. Her Tudor manor, tucked away in Worcestershire, boasted a whole rainbow of chambers. They had been left at Sheila's sole disposal since her children moved out and her husband passed away. Servants had prepared a splendid meal, serving it with a bottle of the late Mitchell Vincent's claret and then making a discreet exit. After a few drinks, Sheila was hanging on his every word and gazing into his eyes.

Of course, he recognised the ringtone. It was Mack the Knife, which he'd thought amusing when he added McPherson to his contacts. He didn't find it so funny anymore.

"Sorry, I'll have to take it. Business," he said.

The corners of her mouth turned down. "I'll get these things cleared up. See you in the blue room."

Naturally, she meant she'd ring for a servant. Sheila didn't exert herself except in the gym. She believed in honing her body relentlessly before she joined her equally rich friends for a ladies' lunch. Afterwards, she'd do nothing more exhausting than shop for cruisewear. Perhaps he'd missed a trick. Once Sheila was history, he should go on a cruise to meet more wealthy widows.

He nodded to her and spoke briefly to McPherson, saying he couldn't talk and would ring back in two minutes. Sheila flounced off, hips wiggling in a tight black dress. It suited her figure and long blonde hair, but the colour did no favours to her lined skin. Forty years ago, the style would have been stunning on her. You only needed to see her daughter to know it. That young woman was much more his type, but he was smart enough to look rather than touch.

Making his way to Mitch's library, the hairs on his neck prickled. The manor house, with its endless wood-panelled corridors, unsettled him nearly as much as McPherson. You could easily get lost. Not usually superstitious, he half expected a ghost to spring from an undiscovered priest hole. Would it be Mitch himself, or a phantom of an earlier vintage?

Since Mitch's death, no-one used the library. Sheila merely read blockbusters picked up at airports. The huge, bay-windowed space, lined with bookshelves, stood dark and silent. He switched on the light, revealing business texts neatly separated from leather-bound Shakespeare.

Ignoring the chesterfield couches, he paced across the Persian carpet. It was vital to stand for the call, to appear assertive and strong. Finally, he jabbed the screen to dial back.

"What took you so long? I—"

"I know, I know," he interrupted. "Do accept my apologies. You'll get your money."

"It was due yesterday. Tell me why I shouldn't break your legs?" McPherson's voice carried a cockney undertone. That twang had made him feel superior when they were introduced at the races, as had McPherson's flashy Rolex. He recognised his mistake now. McPherson's success as an entrepreneur was built on an unconventional approach.

He shuddered, imagining McPherson in front of him, guzzling a brandy even finer than Sheila's Armagnac and blowing cigar smoke in his face. The stink of it always sent a surge of bile to his throat. You might overlook it when you were buddies, blowing cash on the horses together, but not when you were on the wrong end of a business deal.

"Well? You're not convincing me," McPherson said.

"Can we agree an instalment plan? Twenty thousand pounds first thing tomorrow."

"Sure. And twenty grand for each of the next ten weeks."

There was no point in working out the interest rate. It would be exorbitant. "Done," he said.

"You're more sensible than you look," McPherson told him. "Ciao. And don't forget: first thing, okay?"

He stared at the phone long after McPherson cut the call. Where would he find twenty grand quickly? Not everyone had Sheila Vincent's luck, sinking her polished talons into a captain of industry and inheriting half of his considerable estate on his death. She must have millions in the bank. It was her sole attraction.

If only he didn't have a rival for her affections. It had been a shock to realise he wasn't alone in hoping to whisk Sheila down the aisle again. He wondered if the other fellow also intended, carefully and untraceably, to send her to her grave afterwards.

It was proving a longer game than expected, but the prize was worth it. His debts were outweighed in value by the very rug beneath his feet. Some of those unloved books would be priceless too. Apart from the Shakespeare, the surrounding shelves accommodated rows of signed first editions. Tomorrow, he'd spirit a few of them away and visit an antiquarian dealer. He faced an unpleasant, and possibly short, future if he couldn't lay his hands on more funds. McPherson, while his most vocal creditor, was not alone.

Sheila sashayed into the library, to be greeted by his most winning smile. "All taken care of," he said. "Deals and deadlines, huh? Goes with the territory, I'm afraid."

She pouted, not a sexy look, although she might believe it was. "Mitch never switched off either. Except... well, there's the brat."

"Ah." He arranged his features into a semblance of sympathy. "His love child."

"Love had nothing to do with it. Mitch just couldn't keep his trousers on for five minutes." Her face was ugly with scorn, her gaze intense. "And now she's inheriting a fortune, money that should have gone to my children."

He maintained a poker face. Her children were receiving fortunes too: the family business was going to the eldest and the others would have two million pounds each. He hadn't heard them complaining about it.

"I've been researching probate law," Sheila announced, lips settling into a half-smile. "Suppose the brat had an unfortunate accident and died without a will? Did you know my darlings would get everything she owns?"

"Of course," he murmured, as he made it his business to know such things, "but it isn't likely to happen, is it?"

"It could. I had a private investigator check up on her. A husband or children, even parents, would usually inherit, but she's not married. No kids. And her mother, the conniving bitch, died several years ago. I'm waiting to find out if there's a will. Is that something you can establish?"

"I should think so. But it would be unusual for a single twenty-something to bother, especially if she wasn't aware of her windfall yet. And what makes you think a healthy young girl would suffer an untimely death?"

"I'm sure it can be arranged." She smirked, thrusting her wrinkled cleavage towards him.

She was quite mad. Being charitable, it was the wine talking, a sumptuous St-Emilion. He forced himself to appear delighted, even curious, allowing a slow grin to emerge. "I rather feel it's best to say no more. That comment is capable of being misinterpreted."

Sheila's smile slipped. "But you have contacts, don't you? You come across all sorts in your profession. Don't you know people who could make it happen?"

He did, McPherson being one of them, but why should he do a lunatic's dirty work? It was risky to kill too often.

"I could pay," she said. "A lot."

He stiffened. His glance fell on the bookshelves. The brat should pray their contents were as valuable as he suspected.

# CHAPTER 4

## JENNA

Sam had moved quickly. Within twenty-four hours of the bailiff's visit, I had a Zoom call scheduled with Ashleigh, his brother's fiancée. Sam offered to hold the fort too. Although I'd popped to the café at 6am to bake for the day, I'd returned home once he arrived.

I checked my appearance in the ornate mirror above the fireplace. The gold frame, festooned with flowers and cherubs, represented a victory over Ned's minimalist tastes. So did the purple velvet sofa positioned by the window to overlook the suspension bridge. Ned had had the last laugh, though. Every stick of furniture he'd bought had been shipped out when he left. I'd cadged a few dark wood pieces and painted them in bright colours, but the flat still seemed bare.

The image in the mirror felt like a defeat too. My fifties-style makeup had been toned down for the Zoom call: no red lipstick or cat-eyes this morning. I wore a sensible navy jumper, a go-to garment for my graduate job in insurance. Having sworn never to be a corporate clone again, I hated the look.

I smoothed down my dark hair and pinned it back, stealing swigs from a mug of weak instant coffee. Vincent's aromatic beans were a luxury reserved for the café. Perhaps it was just as well. Already jittery, I didn't need the extra caffeine sending me into overdrive.

Laptop plugged in, I fidgeted on the sofa, staring at the bridge. I'd decided to keep it in my sight during the call, reminding me how much I longed to stay in Clifton. Nervously, I logged into Ashleigh's virtual meeting room. A pop-up advised me that I was waiting for my host. Seconds later, she admitted me.

Ashleigh wore a businesslike black jacket and her flaxen hair scraped into a bun. Her face smiled at the screen, a vision of fake lashes, powder, and fuchsia-pink gloss. The plentiful cosmetics didn't disguise her natural prettiness, nor her youth. She looked much younger than Sam and me. I wondered if she really was a mortgage expert. Sam's brother took no notice of the law; he wouldn't be fussed if he'd hooked up with a scammer.

"Good morning, Jenna!" Ashleigh bubbled with enthusiasm. "I've heard so much about you from Ryan. You're the girl who tempted Sam to the big city."

I stiffened at the hint that Sam and I were a couple. Why would she imagine that? "You're bigging up my role. Sam just happened to get into the Bristol Old Vic Theatre School at the same time I started uni here. It was great to have a friend in town, of course."

"Yes, I've heard all about student life." She pouted. "Sometimes I'm sorry I missed out, but never mind. I chose a different path and it worked out."

"What did you do?"

"Straight into an apprenticeship at eighteen. A nine to five job combined with studying every evening, so no social life. No student loan hanging around my neck either, though. Now I'm a qualified mortgage broker at twenty-one. You would not believe how busy it's been since the mini-budget last week. Interest rates went crazy. You're not alone in wanting to refinance. My clients have been ringing me non-stop."

My stomach churned at the harsh truth I'd been avoiding. Loans had suddenly become more expensive just when I'd run out of options.

Ashleigh continued. "I work with Kilpatricks. Have you heard of them?"

I had. They were a respected firm of financial advisers, with branches all over the UK. "I had dealings with them in my previous job. After uni, I went into insurance."

I'd grown to love Bristol during my history degree course, and couldn't believe my luck when I found a well-paid graduate job in the city centre. The work had been soul-destroying, but how I missed my monthly salary.

"Anyway, let's talk about you." Ashleigh flashed her perfect white teeth again. "You own a small business now, don't you? That's what I love about Ryan and his friends. You're all so entrepreneurial. So let's discuss your finance needs. Tell me how I can help."

There was admiration rather than irony in her voice. Ryan's cavalier approach to the law clearly didn't bother her, but I resented being grouped with him in her mind. It wasn't as if I shoplifted my cupcake ingredients. I'd be in a much stickier mess if I had.

Taking a deep breath, I considered how to sum up my problems in a few words. "I set up Jenna's Cupcakery at the start of 2020. It's a vintage-style café in Clifton."

"Near the suspension bridge?"

"A couple of streets away, but you can see the bridge from my flat." I stole a furtive glance at it. Sunlight reflected off the graceful metal structure.

"You're so lucky," Ashleigh said. "Do you own the property?"

"Yes, although there's a mortgage on it. At a fixed rate but that runs out next month." I shuddered. Thanks to my employer, I'd had a fantastic deal. This was precisely the wrong time to be making changes, let alone borrowing more to fend off the bailiffs.

"You're in the best area of Bristol," Ashleigh said briskly. "I'm confident I can do something for you. We can discuss specifics later."

She was twenty-one going on forty. A twinge of guilt told me I'd misjudged her because of her links to Sam's flaky family. It was easy to divine what Ryan saw in her, but she could have done better. Presumably, she liked his cheeky chappie charm.

"Do carry on," Ashleigh prompted.

"I expected the café to do well from the get-go. There are at least a dozen coffee shops in Clifton Village," I recalled what the gym buddy had told Sam, "but there are hundreds of coffee drinkers, too, and my concept was unique for Bristol. My ex worked in London and he said cupcakes did well there. It didn't happen, though. I'd hardly opened the doors when the pandemic started. We went into lockdown. I borrowed sixty thousand pounds from my ex and he wants it back."

Ned had given me money whenever I needed it. He'd paid for the premises to be fitted out, and for my living costs when he shared my flat during the lockdowns. Delivering cupcakes and selling takeaways hadn't kept the wolf from my door. I'd been grateful for his help.

The only problem was that it hadn't been a gift.

How had I been so stupid? Last night, I'd forced myself to open the pile of post I'd ignored. Ned had made increasingly strained demands for payment, and he'd attached copies of loan documents. I hardly remembered signing them. During the pandemic, I'd drunk more than usual – we both had - and he'd waved paperwork in front of me for a signature from time to time.

If I'd gone to court, I might have been able to fight back. Unfortunately, I'd ignored the letter summoning me to a hearing, and others explaining that judgement had been given against me.

"My business brain turned to mush when he left. I stuck my head in the sand," I admitted to Ashleigh. "All my bills have gone up, my business has lost money, and I've maxed out my credit cards. Now my ex has a CCJ against me. I've got to repay him, and roll over the borrowings on my flat too."

I gripped the sides of my laptop. At any minute, Ashleigh would roll her eyes and say sorry, the situation was hopeless.

Her smile barely wavered. "A CCJ limits your options," she announced. "A lot. Still, I'm sure I can help, especially with the equity in your flat. Can you talk me through your income and outgoings?"

I gulped. It was already a grim picture. Each month, I spent more than I earned. Utility bills had rocketed, as had my raw material costs. The café wasn't busy enough to pay for itself.

Ashleigh listened patiently, asking an occasional question.

"You need to cut your costs," she said. "No more spa visits or foreign holidays. Do your weekly shop at Aldi rather than Waitrose. It's not forever, just until your finances are in better shape."

At this point, I suspected she'd read from a script. Spas, sun-seeking and high-end supermarkets weren't part of the life I'd described to her. I was struggling to stand still, much less make aspirational purchases.

"Look for income too," Ashleigh chirped. "Can you sell your car?"

"I'd get nothing for it." Sadie was a baby-pink Fiat 500, high on cuteness and low in value. Her name had followed her from her third owner. She represented freedom as well as convenience. Without her, a trip to the cash and carry would be almost impossible. Even the nearest discount supermarket, a breeze in the car, was a nightmare by public transport or a thirty-minute walk down a steep hill and across a river.

"Cars are dear to run. Do you really need one in the city?" Evidently noticing my mulish expression, Ashleigh moved on. "Do you have a spare room? You could take a lodger or Airbnb it."

I was barely holding it together. Otherwise, I'd have laughed at the irony of going back to my roots, stripping sheets and preparing breakfast for guests. There was no way I could combine it with my duties at the café.

I blinked away a tear. "It's hopeless. I can't even get by at the moment. How will I cope when I'm paying twice as much interest?"

Ashleigh stayed perky. She muttered soothing words and listed practical ideas. I should keep my existing mortgage, because even when the interest rate rose, it would be lower than the deals she could secure for me with a judgement outstanding. To pay Ned, she suggested a second mortgage.

"It will be expensive," she cautioned, "but you can mitigate that. You can add the arrangement fees to the loan principal, request an interest-only option and opt for a forty-year term. That's totally possible at your age."

"The sums don't add up, though," I said. "I won't be able to meet the payments."

Ashleigh nodded. "On current income, that's right, but you're buying yourself time. You've got plenty of equity, so I recommend borrowing twenty thousand pounds more than you need. It will give you a breathing space, because you can use it to fund the gaps between income and expenditure until you find a structural solution."

"Which would be?"

"Well, there are several alternatives. The most obvious answer is to close your café unless you can stop it losing money. Like I said, it's not forever. Get a job and rebuild your bank balance. You can go self-employed again when you're in a better place. Who knows, you may like what you're doing and decide to stay."

I crossed my arms, hugging myself. With the café, I was keeping Mum's memory alive, especially when I baked recipes we'd tried out together. We'd spent weeks perfecting her Black Forest cupcakes. Sam swore they were the best he'd ever tasted. How could I give it up to go back to an office?

I recalled long and stressful days at the insurance company. Listening to Ashleigh reminded me how much I'd hated the jargon and the pressure to appear upbeat when I was dying inside. My only friend was Beth, who had started on the graduate trainee programme at the same time. We became adept at finding tiny gaps in our schedules to sneak out for wine at the Spoons pub nearby. That alone made our work tolerable.

Beth and I were still best buddies, especially as I'd been a matchmaker for her and Sam. They lived together in her cosy cottage, to which I frequently invited myself with a bottle of wine. Only last week, chatting over Pinot Grigio, she'd mentioned my former employers were recruiting. They wished I'd return. The door was open, but could I bear to enter it?

"Or you could sell your flat," Ashleigh said.

My eyes flicked away from her screen to the iconic view framed in my window. I stifled a sob.

"You needn't make a decision now," Ashleigh said kindly. "I'll run some figures and get you a quote later today. I can recommend a lawyer too. Mr Speedy, I call him. He'll get the paperwork sorted super-fast and we'll roll up his fees into the loan. How does that sound?"

"Great," I managed.

She wished me a cheery farewell. We had spent exactly twenty-eight minutes on the call and she undoubtedly had another client waiting to be saved from financial doom.

Switching off the laptop, I let myself cry, clutching a cushion to my chest for comfort. "Sorry Mum," I whispered.

Colours flashed through the bridge's railings as cars drove across. Everyone was going about their daily lives, chasing their dreams, while mine were crumbling.

# CHAPTER 5

## JENNA

"Jenna, how are you?"

I jumped at the familiar voice, turning to find Andrew right behind me. The door shut with a clang. He must have been approaching even as I flipped the sign from CLOSED to OPEN.

I returned his warm smile. October rain might fall outside, but the sun must shine in Jenna's Cupcakery. It would be foolish to admit I was on edge, devastated by the collapse of my dreams. Soon I'd have a cushion of extra cash, though, and a month or so to decide on my future. Ashleigh had delivered on her promises. She and Peter, her Mr Speedy, had worked tirelessly to ensure Ned would receive his money next week.

On Fridays, we weren't exactly rushed off our feet, but I missed Sam. I could have used his gentle empathy. However, he'd gone to London for an audition, so I was working solo. It was a relief to see Andrew's friendly face. I'd been afraid the bailiffs had scared him off; he hadn't been to the café since their visit on Monday.

"How are you, Andrew? Would you like your usual flat white? And I'm whipping up lemon cupcakes this morning, so I'd love to hear what you think of them."

"They'll be scrummy, guaranteed."

As his eyes met mine, a jolt of desire sparked into life. Flustered, I sprang back from him.

"What's wrong? Sorry, Jenna, I didn't mean to invade your space. I've just been worried about you." He claimed his usual table by setting his laptop bag down on it. "I would have dropped by before, but I had to return to the Midlands to stop World War 3 breaking out."

"I'm okay." I beamed at him. "How was your trip?"

He clearly didn't want to tell me, and he wasn't fooled by my fake cheeriness. "Life is tough for small businesses like ours, isn't it?" he said. "Listen, if you need a sympathetic ear, I'm here for you."

I retreated behind the counter, warmth creeping over my neck. From the minute he'd first walked into the café, I'd clocked Andrew as hot, and now it seemed he was kind too. It would serve me well to keep our boundaries professional, though. As a customer, Andrew came here for coffee rather than a relationship.

He sat down, opened his laptop, and immediately became engrossed in it. I peeked at him over the espresso machine. His well-pressed white shirt hinted at appointments later. Perhaps I should suggest he used the café for his business meetings. He'd never be able to have a private conversation in such a tiny space, though. The pink walls and bunting weren't a particularly professional setting, either. I'd set out to attract a female clientele, and Andrew's loyalty came as a welcome surprise.

We were on first name terms but I didn't know much about him. At a guess, he was in his late thirties, so he undoubtedly had baggage. While he didn't wear a ring, he could still be married. Maybe he was gay. My heart sank at the thought.

He tutted at the screen, opened his laptop bag, and placed a couple of glossy brochures on the table.

I couldn't stop myself from glancing at them as I delivered his drink. They were estate agents' particulars for villas in Cliftonwood, the area stretching down the Avon Gorge from Clifton to the river. Its streets were especially picturesque as the terraced houses had been rendered and painted in different colours.

"They're pretty," I said. "I'm sure I went to a party in that yellow house as a student."

"Well, you wouldn't recognise it now. It's been tarted up for sale. Have a look." He handed me the booklet.

I fingered the thick, shiny card. The photos revealed cream carpets, muted shades, and a complete absence of personality. Ned would have approved.

Andrew noticed my lack of enthusiasm. "Not your style, is it? Nor mine, but as I said, it's been refurbished for a quick sale."

"Are you an estate agent?" I asked.

"No, I'm in the market as a buyer. Annoyingly, prices are going up. I hoped they'd drop with the credit squeeze." He winced. "Sorry, that wasn't very tactful, was it? Anyhow, you asked about my work. I'm an IT consultant. My biggest client is here in Clifton. They don't have a desk for me, but they like me to be available at short notice. It's a pain."

"I can imagine," I said, recalling last-minute panics at the office.

"You don't need to hear about my woes, though, do you? I'm guessing you have enough of your own. Did everything work out on Monday? You bet I was pleased to find you were still here."

A lump in my throat stopped me replying. I nodded.

"Tell me about it if you like," Andrew said. "Sometimes, it helps to talk it out. I might even have a few ideas. You know, I've been round the block a few times myself." He gestured to the chair beside him.

"Those lemon cupcakes won't bake themselves." I forced out a grin, then sat beside him. There were no other customers around yet.

Andrew closed his laptop. "You have my full attention. What did those muppets want?"

Despite my predicament, I managed a half-smile. He was clearly on my team. "I made some bad decisions and took out loans I shouldn't have, but that's all sorted now. I'm remortgaging. The trouble is, I don't think I can afford the payments. I'll have to close the café and get a job."

He looked horrified. "That would be terrible. I'll lose my favourite café. My flat is so tiny, I go stir-crazy as soon as I wake up." His hand reached towards mine and then withdrew. He'd obviously thought better of it. "I'm sorry, Jenna, I'm being selfish. You must be gutted."

"Yes." I sniffed. "This has been my dream for years. I didn't go into it carelessly, either. I had costings, market research. It all stacked up, but then the pandemic—"

This time, he patted my hand. "Say no more. Covid and the cost of living crisis have sent thousands of firms under. You can be proud that you kept going."

"Not for much longer."

"Don't say that. You mentioned a mortgage. Can you sell this place and open a stall instead, or a van? I've seen several in the city centre."

"No. I rent the café. The landlord was flexible to start with, but not anymore. I own a flat and that's how I was able to borrow."

"Well, sell that and downsize. Unless, like mine, it's only a pied-à-terre." He grinned. "That's what estate agents call it, but it's less a foot on the ground than a toehold."

Moisture prickled my eyes. "I adore my flat as much as the café. Clifton is the nicest place I've ever lived. I've even got views over the suspension bridge."

Andrew whistled. "I understand why you want to stay. Listen, how big is your apartment?"

"A good size for Clifton." I had a duplex in a double-fronted house.

"How many bedrooms?"

"Two, and a boxroom."

"In that case, I have an idea," Andrew said. "Maybe we can help each other. Could I—"

The door opened, admitting a gust of chilly air and two thirtysomething women with pushchairs.

"I'll tell you later," Andrew said. "Let me buy you dinner tonight."

I found myself agreeing. What would I lose?

One of the newcomers waved at me. "Do you have a couple of highchairs, please?"

"Fortunately, I have exactly two. And we do babycinos or juice for the little ones."

"Perfect."

I made their skinny soy lattes, while Andrew advised the women to try the freshly baked cakes; they wouldn't regret it. Although he hadn't even sampled the batch I'd baked before his arrival, his pitch was persuasive. He was almost as eloquent a salesman as Sam.


Rain started lashing the café windows ten minutes before Andrew returned. Any customers were long gone. I'd closed at five, and if I hadn't been meeting him, I'd have hurried home then. Instead, after surfing for recipes on my phone, I vacuumed for a second time and buffed up the coffee maker's chrome finish.

A large puddle had formed outside the door, its surface roiling from the splashes my mother called 'dancers in the water'. I was grateful for my vintage polka dot raincoat. As I locked up, I saw Andrew waiting under a large black umbrella. I smiled. It was unlikely that he'd solve my problems, but I could forget about them for a few hours. He was sure to be good company.

Andrew moved closer to share his brolly. "Sorry, Jenna," he said. "I tried for a table at the Ivy, but they had nothing before nine."

"I can't say I'm surprised. It's the best place in Clifton Village." I tried to hide my disappointment. The brasserie was part of an upmarket chain, and I adored its maximalist décor. Their cocktails hit the spot too. Beth and I had been regulars there when we first worked together and had no-one waiting for us at home. She'd crash out at my place after a long evening, and we'd return to the restaurant for brunch.

The happy memories lifted my mood again. "Where are we going then?" I asked him.

"That's the problem. Friday night is so busy. I've discovered the hard way that you have to book ahead for anywhere that's a little bit special.

And take it from me, Jenna, special is what you deserve. But I'm no mean cook, if I say so myself. I've got a boeuf bourguignon bubbling away and a fantastic bottle of red to go with it. How about it?"

"You mean, at your flat?" I shrank from him. Andrew was virtually a stranger. Being alone with him on his own territory was a different proposition from a meal in a public place.

"Listen." Andrew's gaze fixed mine. "I get why you're alarmed but rest assured, I'm harmless. I want you to be comfortable around me. If it will help, phone a friend. Tell them where you're going and give them my address. Here, hang onto my keys if you're scared I'll lock you in."

He thrust a bundle of jingling metal into my hand. A Tesla logo adorned the key ring.

I giggled to disguise my nerves. "Well, if that's okay. What's the address?"

It turned out to be down the road, where a small courtyard of Georgian terraces opened out from the street. I texted Beth, then handed the keys back to Andrew. "I trust you."

"That's a relief. Come along and join me at the feast. Did I mention there's chocolate too?"

He lived in a tall, thin house. We walked up three flights of stairs, footsteps resounding on wipe-clean flooring. The halls and stairwell were painted cream, with two or three Yale-locked doors on each level. It seemed impersonal. The only signs of life were mingled smells of stale curry and the chemical odour of cheap air freshener. They gave way to a delicious aroma as we reached the last floor.

"Welcome to my humble abode," Andrew said, unlocking the door. He ushered me inside. "That stew needs a glug of wine, and so do we. Make yourself at home."

I sat on a squarish brown leather sofa and took in my surroundings. His flat was minute, its whitewashed walls failing to give an illusion of space. Although lacking much furniture, it felt crowded. A folding metal table and two chairs, the sort you might find on a patio, were set up in front of the window. Nearby, a run of kitchen units was topped with a hob, work surface, and sink. Another door presumably led to a bathroom. I deliberately averted my eyes from the corner where the bed had been squeezed in. Andrew seemed harmless, but I didn't want to give him ideas.

He flashed me an anxious glance. "Not what you expected? Now you know why I'm eager to spread my wings in a coffee shop."

"You did warn me your place was small."

"It met my needs until now." He opened a bottle of red wine, tipping about a third into the saucepan sitting on the hob and splitting the rest between two glasses. Handing one to me, he slouched against the table, watching as I took a sip.

"Like it?" he asked.

"Very nice," I said automatically. The wine was fruity and warming, perfect for an autumn day. I stretched my legs to overcome an urge to fidget. Something about his stare set me on edge again.

Andrew knocked back half of his glass. "I'll cut to the chase. This studio is too small. I bought it years ago as an investment. Skye always liked Bristol—"

"Sky?" I asked, confused.

"My daughter. S-K-Y-E. I used to bring her to the city to visit relatives near the university. She said she wanted to go there when she grew up. Well, when I saw this flat in an auction, I snapped it up. I figured it was a good deal whether she went to Bristol or not."

"How old is Skye?" It was a surprise to find Andrew had a daughter contemplating university. He seemed too youthful for that.

"She's fourteen and wise beyond her years." He grinned ruefully. "It wasn't my plan to start a family so young, but I will honestly say she's the best thing that ever happened to me. Hopefully, you'll meet her, and you'll agree. She's absolutely sensational."

A wave of empathy engulfed me. It was refreshing to hear a man speak so movingly about his child. Richard merely viewed me as a nuisance and a source of free labour. He'd rarely had a kind word for me. As for my real father, who knew what he might have said? I didn't have a clue who he was, and that told its own story.

"I didn't imagine I'd end up living here," Andrew continued. "But I took on a client in Bristol and they insisted I relocate. There were troubles in my marriage, too. My wife and I had agreed to separate. It made sense for me to come here and give her space. I should have realised how awful it would be for Skye. My wife isn't a nice person and Skye is desperate to get away from her."

"Is that why you went back to the north?"

"To the Midlands. Yes. Listen, I'll tell you more in a minute, but we really should eat. Move over to the table and I'll dish up. More wine?"

He opened a wall cupboard and produced another bottle of red.

"Please." I parked myself gingerly on a folding seat, slats digging into my bottom. It would be rude to complain, especially as Andrew had made such an effort. The table was already set. In the centre, a single pink rose billowed over the edge of a miniature vase. Andrew left the bottle beside it after topping up our glasses.

He served the plates of stew with slices of crusty bread. "Dig in."

I tried a forkful. "Delicious."

He exhaled. "Phew. I'm glad you like it. My wife had constant complaints about my cooking. She's verbally abusive. Physically too. I had her word that she wouldn't touch Skye. She's broken that promise."

I didn't reply. Awkwardly, I cast my eyes downwards and took another mouthful of beef.

Andrew carried on over-sharing. "I didn't want to remove Skye from a school where she's settled, but I have no choice. She ran away from home on Tuesday. I tracked her down, but she's not prepared to go back."

"Where is she?" I suddenly realised I was focusing on Andrew's problems rather than my own. Seized by an impulse to comfort him, I touched the back of his hand. It was disturbingly pleasant to feel the silkiness of his fine blond hairs and the warmth of his skin.

"Skye is with a friend," he said softly. "It's a temporary measure. She's going to move to Bristol to be with me. But we can't stay here together, can we?"

Removing my hand from his, I gulped. I sensed where this was leading.

"I'm looking for a bigger property, but it takes months for a purchase to go through. I've hit on the answer, though. If I rent two rooms from you, I'd be doing us both a favour."

He wasn't gay, but I'd been right to suspect complications in his life. I imagined Andrew's wife, who sounded mentally unstable, driving to Bristol and knocking on my door. A quiver ran through my stomach. Appetite gone, I set my fork down. "You mentioned relatives near here. Can't the two of you stay with them?"

"If only." Andrew sighed. "Sadly, my aunt and uncle passed away several years ago. I've got to find somewhere else quickly. But this would work for you too, right? Listen, I'll pay whatever you ask. In cash. No need to tell the taxman, eh?"

I couldn't look him in the eye. Although I needed money, an inner voice asked how I'd cope with the hassle. "I'm sorry, I don't really have enough space. There are two bedrooms, but one of them is mine. And the boxroom is miniscule. I used it as a study during lockdown, but I can't fit much more than a desk in it."

"I could jam a single mattress in there, or sleep standing up. Skye should have a bedroom. She mustn't suffer any more than she already has." Andrew leaned forward, despair etched on his features. "I don't mind keeping it flexible, just one week at a time. Please, Jenna. If you don't help, I can't vouch for my daughter's safety."

# CHAPTER 6

## JENNA

I longed to know how Sam's audition had gone, but in the stress of the last week, I'd forgotten he wouldn't be in on Saturday. It was Beth's birthday, and he'd promised to spend it with her.

Working solo again meant I'd save another day of his pay. Weekends were busy. In spite of the exhausting pace, I enjoyed the vibe. Clifton Village buzzed with visitors. Both locals and tourists came to see and be seen, browsing in the boutiques, and stopping for refreshments. Every table in the café was occupied. Hipsters, students and pensioners chatted over their cupcakes. This was everything I'd dreamed about: a happy place, bringing people together. A profit was virtually guaranteed too.

"Where's Sam this morning?" The gym bunny had taken a seat by the window. Beside her, a lean and sculpted black woman nursed a bulletproof coffee. Both wore similar clothes, with a pricy brand's logo on the waistband.

"He's got the day off," I said.

When she replied that was a pity, she'd told her friend he was cute, I congratulated myself on keeping his relationship out of the conversation. I had no shame about pimping Sam out to gain custom.

Before I could leave the pair to their drinks, the gymgoer nudged her friend. "Hey, Martha, come back soon if you want to check him out. They're closing down."

"We're open for the foreseeable future," I said stiffly.

Behind the counter again, my eyes glistened with unshed tears. I'd lied of course, but she knew the truth. The café's closure was a matter of when, not if. I'd be heartbroken to lose it.

There was Andrew's offer to consider, though. His money would buy me more time. If I could limp on until December, I'd crush it with Christmas cupcakes. I'd be crazy to turn him down. Why would his wife travel all the way to Bristol, anyway? She was aware that Andrew and Skye hated her. I'd been overthinking this.

Andrew had pressed his phone number on me last night, although I'd made excuses and left before the 'delectable chocolate mousse' he promised. He had named a figure too, above market rates for a flat share, but he'd said beggars couldn't be choosers and he wanted to live with someone Skye would adore.

Rushing to fulfil a wave of orders, I finally had ten seconds to spare for a call. It went to voicemail. "The answer is yes, Andrew," I said, asking him to ring to discuss details.

Luckily, my hands were free when he did so. With an apology, I broke away from taking an order, fumbling to reach the phone.

"Can we talk later?" I asked.

"No need. I'm delighted and Skye, let me tell you, is thrilled. We'll move in tomorrow."

I nearly dropped the handset.

Andrew must have sensed my hesitation, because he added, "I would have done it today, but Skye wants to stay another night with her friend. They may not see other again, so I hope that's all right?"

"It's a bit early, if I'm honest," I said. "I'll need references from you. Then there's the paperwork, isn't there? You haven't even viewed the flat."

"I'm sure it will be utterly charming, like your café."

I needed his money too much to argue, but I still felt a quiver of unease. "Can you give me a few days, please?"

"I'm too worried about my daughter to wait. Listen, what's your email address, Jenna? I'll send you a draft contract, and references, today. You can ring them this evening. They'll be fine; I can tell you that. Then I'll pop round to the café tomorrow lunchtime, pay the first week's rent, and pick up the keys. Sounds like a plan?"

"Okay." The offer of cash trumped my reluctance.

A line of customers had appeared during the short call. The hours passed in a blur again. I'd been in early to bake Black Forest, lemon drizzle, and carrot cupcakes, but all had gone by 3pm, apart from mistakes with wobbly icing. If a cake was less than perfect, I wouldn't sell it. Sam usually took defective baked goods away, although he couldn't possibly eat them all. He gave them to friends, flatmates, and even rough sleepers he passed on the street.

With the cakes gone, my sweet-toothed guests had to make do with fruit infusions. A pot of mango and strawberry tea was brewing when Sam and Beth walked in, rosy-cheeked and excited. Both her short dark crop and his long blond straggle had been swept back from their faces by the wind.

"Happy Birthday, Beth. What a lovely surprise. Did Sam give you my card?"

"Of course. And the chocolate lollipop. I had it for breakfast."

"It was just a little something." I blushed. She still bought me the sort of fancy present we'd found for each other when we worked together, but I couldn't afford to reciprocate. I made small bursts of deliciousness instead.

Beth slipped behind the counter, enfolding me in a hug and kissing my cheeks. "It was an incredible breakfast. Sam brought it to me in bed."

For a second, I fantasised about Andrew doing so for me. Then I snapped out of it. "I love your scarf," I said. It was long and silky, in a red rose print, quite unlike the black and grey shades she usually wore. The contrast suited her dark hair.

"Thanks. It was a gift from Sam."

"Not the only one. I'm taking her on a tour of Clifton Village, and there's a goodie for her whenever we stop."

"I'm paying you too much," I protested, although if it had been any less, I'd have broken the law.

"Charity shops," Sam said in a stage whisper. "Whatever, we've come to a halt in the world's finest cupcakery, so—" He retrieved a tiny square box from his pocket.

It had that black velvet finish typical of fine jewellers. I gasped. At last, he'd done it. Beth had been hinting for so long that she wanted a long-term commitment from him. I was overjoyed for her.

Beth's green eyes sparkled. She took the box from him carefully, as if handling a piece of fragile porcelain. Slowly, she flicked it open.

Inside, there was a jade pendant in the shape of a Chinese dragon.

"That's cute."

I could see her trying to be mature about it and hide her dismay. Sam was usually so intuitive; I was amazed he didn't notice.

"It's the colour of your eyes, Beth. How lovely." I hoped she wouldn't realise I'd known she expected a ring. After all, I'd thought the same.

This wasn't the time or place to scold him for his tactlessness. Instead, I offered them both coffee on the house and a bag of cake mistakes.

The afternoon had reached that point where dusk hadn't yet fallen but the sun's light was dimming. Spotting a free table by the window, I suggested they sit there. After making their drinks, I placed a tealight on a saucer in front of them.

"We need a sugar rush," Sam said. "Here." He blew out the candle, carefully placed it to one side and emptied pieces of Black Forest cupcake onto the saucer. Grabbing a teaspoon, he fed Beth cherries and cream. It amused the other customers, and she seemed to relax again.

"Busy day?" he asked me.

"You bet. A good one, though. I survived without you. You brought my bestie to see me. And I've solved my financial crisis."

"Awesome. How did you do that?"

"You remember Andrew Maxwell?"

"Who?"

"He was sitting over there when it kicked off on Monday." I jerked a thumb at his regular spot by the counter.

"That's his name, is it?" Sam's lips tightened. "What of him, anyway?"

"He and his daughter will be lodging with me, as of tomorrow. The rent will keep me solvent."

Sam blanched. "Are you sure you want him living with you? There's something weird about that guy."

"How do you mean?" I asked.

"I can't put my finger on it, but he seems off." After a long pause, he added, "I've noticed him staring at you. And once, when I brought him a coffee, he snapped his laptop shut. I bet he was looking at porn."

"Wouldn't he do that in private?" Beth laughed, her smile freezing as she noted the horrified expression on his face.

"Andrew was probably working on a business deal. Or browsing properties. Our arrangement is short-term. He's trying to buy a house, and it's only until he gets somewhere."

"Please don't do it, Jenna," Sam said.

"What choice have I got? I'm broke."

Bile rose in my throat. Sam was right. I didn't have to share my home with a shifty, secretive man, a troubled adolescent girl, and the spectre of a violent wife. I could tell Andrew I'd changed my mind, then plan a swift exit from my business. The gym bunny's prophecy would come to pass, because without Andrew, my dreams were dust.

I loved my little café too much to let it go, though. Whatever Sam thought, Andrew and Skye Maxwell would be moving in tomorrow.

# CHAPTER 7

## JENNA

Amazingly, Sam didn't have a hangover when he turned up for work on Sunday. We opened later at weekends, so he'd had more time to recover. I listened with envy as he recounted all the booze he and Beth had poured down their necks the night before.

Proving that he'd planned ahead, they'd enjoyed cocktails at the Ivy. After the first, she'd paid. He admitted that he'd found it emasculating. It frustrated Sam that, apart from his actor friends and me, everyone he knew earned more than him. Even Ryan had moved on from bricklaying to property development, although he'd need to avoid stolen kitchen units in future.

"You just need that one big break," I told him. "Hang on in there. Then you can buy Beth a ring."

Sam grunted. "Maybe. Have you told Andrew to get lost yet?"

"No. I need his money." Did Sam even realise that I'd struggle to pay his wages without Andrew's rent?

Sam sighed. "I don't trust him."

"Well, you should. I'm not worried. I mean, his references were great." It had been a rush, but both Andrew's bank manager and a client were happy to speak on the phone. After a busy day, I'd finally caught up with them in the evening. They'd waved away my apologies about calling at the weekend. Everyone expected twenty-four-seven service, they said. It wasn't just café owners who worked on Saturdays.

Sam wasn't satisfied. "Whatever they told you, you should make an inventory of your valuables."

"What valuables? I don't have any."

"You'd be surprised. Even my mum has bits that go in and out of the pawn shop. My gran's wedding ring, things like that. If you had any jewellery from your mother when she died, you don't want that slimeball nicking it. Then there's your laptop."

"He's got his own."

Sam scowled. "And put a lock on your bedroom door."

I gawped at him. "You're paranoid. His fourteen-year-old daughter will be living with us. Andrew's hardly going to try anything when she's around."

I didn't say chance would be a fine thing. Sam would be unimpressed at the slightest hint that I found Andrew attractive. Still, I would keep Andrew at arm's length, at least until I knew him better.

The door opened. Our first customers of the day had arrived, and to my surprise, it was the gym bunny and Martha.

Sam shifted into actor mode, bounding towards the two women with a broad smile on his face. It was as if they'd switched on a light bulb within him. "How are you, my loves?"

"Ready for a coffee, then I'll shop until I drop," the gym bunny said. "The boutique on Portland Street has the new Grace Vincent collection in their window."

"That's her diffusion range," Martha said. "I saw the real thing at London Fashion Week. Gorgeous dresses. I was in the front row, of course." Her face smug, she scrutinised her friend. "I'd say you might lose a few kilos first. That plissé fabric favours the thin."

The gym bunny's lips tightened. Her eyes widened, the upper lids flickering as if she wanted to move the muscles, but couldn't.

"You'll be fine as you are, believe me," Sam said. "Grace fitted half the stars for my last film premiere. They're no slimmer than you and they were amazing on the red carpet."

"I thought as much," the gym bunny said. "The secret is in the cut."

"Grace is so talented, and such a sweetheart," Sam said. "Jenna, did I tell you about her? She's one of the Vincent's Coffee dynasty, but so down to earth."

Martha peered at me. "You look a bit like Grace. Are you related?"

"I don't think so." I fidgeted, wishing Sam would take their order. More customers had started to arrive.

Sam glanced over. "I see what you mean. Yes, definitely a resemblance, but Jenna is much prettier. Anyway, what would you like? The double chocolate cupcakes are epic."


Andrew turned up at lunchtime, with Skye in tow.

Petite and thin, Skye called to mind a fragile porcelain doll. Her ivory skin glowed, unmarred by the acne which had plagued my adolescence.

Glossy blonde hair tumbled over the shoulders of a blue hoodie which matched the colour of her eyes.

Skye pouted. "How long will this take?" she whined.

Her strong Birmingham accent took me by surprise. Andrew didn't have one; like many successful businessmen, his voice gave no clue to his origins.

His laughter betrayed a nervous edge. "We'll be done in a jiffy, sweetie. I've just got to sort out payment, then you can snuggle down in Jenna's lovely flat and watch Netflix."

"I'm afraid I cancelled my subscription," I said, hoping it wouldn't be a dealbreaker.

Skye stared at me with open contempt. "You don't need a subscription to watch Netflix. Everybody knows that."

"We have our own," Andrew said hastily.

Skye's eyes skimmed the room with its chatting customers and cheery bunting, not bothering to hide her scorn. Then her gaze lit on Sam. She stared, nudging Andrew. "That's Sam Farrow, right? From Call The Marshalls?"

About to reply, I stopped when Sam flashed me a warning glance. The TV series was a sore point with him. He'd pinned all his hopes on the role. Canny country cousin Lucas Marshall wasn't far removed from Sam in real life, even down to the Somerset drawl. Yet, although he'd been an instant hit with the public, Lucas had been written out of the plot after two weeks. It was rumoured that the leading man had insisted on it.

Andrew was distracted. "Probably," he told Skye. "Give me a minute to pay the rent." He removed a stack of credit cards from his wallet.

"I thought you offered to pay cash?" I said, alarmed at the prospect of tax and other hassle when the money went through the business.

"Sorry." Andrew's eyes met mine. "Skye's friends are raising funds for the floods in Pakistan. When they showed me photos of starving orphans, I couldn't say no. It cleaned me out, I'm afraid. I hope you understand."

"How about a bank transfer to my personal account?"

"It won't go through at the weekend. I'd rather pay you now."

"I suppose I can take a card," I said, feeling boxed into a corner.

"Can we split it between cards? Keep it below the contactless limit."

"I guess. It'll take a while, though." I might have been more suspicious if I hadn't become adept at juggling multiple credit cards myself.

Skye occupied herself with her iPhone. "It is him," she hissed. Virtually leaping in front of Sam, she demanded a selfie.

Once he complied, she was all smiles, especially when he suggested going with both of them to my flat to 'check them in.'

"No, I should do that. You cover here," I said.

Skye, clearly disappointed, repeatedly shifted her weight from one foot to the other. Her eyes followed Sam as he schmoozed the customers.

It took a few minutes to process Andrew's payments. He returned the cards to his wallet. "Ready when you are," he said brightly.

A sulky Skye followed us out of the café, slinking into the back seat of a newish BMW parked on double yellow lines outside. There was no environmentally-friendly Tesla in sight. Perhaps his wife had kept it.

Andrew opened the passenger door for me. "We'll drive, shall we? I know it's only round the corner, but our luggage is heavy."

I suspected Sam would have imagined a devilish plot to kidnap me, but I took a seat without blinking. I found the vehicle's tidiness and smell of polish reassuring. Skye's teenage attitude aside, the pair promised to be good tenants.

Thankfully, Andrew managed to find a space for the car two doors from my flat. "Why don't you show us round before I bring the cases in?" he suggested.

I led them up stone steps to the front door, painted white to match the stucco of the house. Seeing him glance at the gracious wrought-iron balcony above, I paused. I'd better manage his expectations. "Sorry, not ours. I've got half the second floor and all the third."

"More stairs then. Well, that's normal for Clifton, I suppose. Built them tall back in the Georgian era," Andrew said, his cheerfulness sounding strained. "I'm sure we'll be happy here, won't we, Skye?"

She didn't answer, remaining silent as I took them into the black and white tiled lobby and up the turned wood staircase, a Berber carpet muffling the sound. The décor in the common parts of the building was a tasteful blend of original features and neutral modern design. Andrew said he liked it. He was chatty, his comments a constant stream of approval.

"How striking," he said when I ushered him into my living room, painted a sunny yellow the week after Ned left. "I really admire your use of colour, Jenna. And what a beautiful view. Look, Skye, there's the bridge."

"You'll see it from your bedroom window too," I told her. "Shall we take a tour?"

I showed them the kitchen at the rear, all dark wood, chrome, and polished granite. It reflected Ned's tastes rather than mine, but I'd been grateful when he paid for tired old units to be replaced. Little did I know I'd signed a loan document. This was the man with whom I'd dreamed of having children. I'd had a lucky escape; Ned cared only for himself.

No-one could have been a better father than Andrew, though. He asked Skye if he should put the kettle on now; she must be tired after the drive from Birmingham and might like a cup of tea.

"I'll make you some when you've done the tour," I said. "Forgive me, I won't stop to have a cuppa with you as I have to get back to the café."

Was it my imagination, or did Skye look relieved?

I pointed out the lavatory tucked away under the stairs, then steered them upwards to the next floor. Here, ceilings were lower, mouldings less ornate, and fireplaces simple cast iron grates. This had been the servants' quarters in bygone days when a rich family occupied the entire house.

"The bedrooms are at the front. That one's mine," I wagged a finger at the stripped pine door, "and here's yours, Skye."

She swept inside, making straight for the small sash window as if I'd lied about the view. Satisfied, she lay sprawling on the double iron bedstead, its duvet dyed to match the turquoise walls I'd stencilled with flowers.

"What's the Wi-Fi like?" They were the first words she'd spoken since her selfie with Sam.

"Fast." Ned would have accepted nothing less.

"Cool. Give me the code, then."

I'd expected her to be more polite after Andrew had raved about her so much. "I'll take you round the rest of the flat first," I said.

"Okay." Skye bounced off the bed, trainers thudding on the bleached floorboards.

"This is for Andrew." I opened the door to the boxroom. "It was my study. I've cleared out the paperwork but I didn't have time to buy a bed for you yet. I'm so sorry."

"Oh dear. I can go to IKEA before they close," Andrew offered.

"There's no need. A single mattress will be delivered tomorrow. I measured the gap next to the desk and it will fit. Meanwhile, the sofa in the living room converts to a bed, so you can sleep there tonight."

"Couch-surfing? You're joking, right?" Skye said, her expression petulant.

"It's fine, honestly," Andrew said. "I appreciate you helping us out, Jenna."

"Those doors are for the bathroom and the airing cupboard. I usually wake around six, so I'd like to take a shower then. I hope that's okay?" It felt weird asking for permission in my own home.

"Works for me," Andrew said. "I can't imagine Skye will be up that early for school, either. Tomorrow, I'll start seeking one out for her. Which is the best around here?"

"Good question." In the café, I'd overheard mothers chatting about schools with an intensity that bordered on obsession. It was a subject I avoided lest it triggered unhappy memories. Racking my brains, I added, "The nearest are miles away, unless you go private. Then there are a couple just across the green, almost next to each other."

"Why do I need to go to school, anyway?" Skye demanded. "I can't believe you're discussing my future as if I'm not even here."

"Sweetie, you're fourteen. It's the law. I'll visit the closest one tomorrow."

"Phone them first," I said. "They may not take new pupils halfway through term."

"I can be persuasive." Andrew winked at me. "How about that cup of tea? If you help me find my way round the kitchen, I'll cook tonight."

"It's better if we cook and eat separately, I think, given our different schedules." I reckoned Skye would be picky about anything I prepared, and I didn't trust her not to lace my food with arsenic.

She did nothing to dispel the impression. "Suits me," she said. "I'll stay up here for now. Can I have the Wi-Fi code?"

"You know how it is with teenagers," Andrew said. "Glued to social media. Instagram, isn't it, Skye?"

She scowled at him in reply.

"My cupcakery is on Instagram. We could follow each other."

"Yeah, right." Skye turned the full force of her glare in my direction. She took out her phone and asked, "Where is it, then?"

I jotted the code down with pen and paper, glad to see her disappear to her room. Following Andrew to the kitchen, I explained where pans, crockery and cutlery were kept. When I left, he was hauling two enormous pink suitcases and one small black one out of the car.

# CHAPTER 8

## SKYE

Dimly aware of a man yelling, Skye removed her AirPods.

"Cup of tea, sweetie?" Andrew marched into her bedroom with a steaming mug.

She laughed. "You're kidding, right? Vodka, please."

"Are you nuts? What's Jenna going to say?"

"Is the bitch still here?"

"No, she went back to work, but I'm not having you sloshed when she comes home. Anyway, I haven't got any booze. You're not raiding hers, either."

"Yes, Dad. Just as well I have my own." She flicked the catches on a bubblegum-coloured Samsonite case. Scrabbling through folded clothes, she retrieved a bottle of Absolut.

"Christ. No wonder it was so heavy. You're a piece of work."

"You love me all the same," she smirked.

"To the moon and back, little girl."

"Then tell me you'll stay clear of that bitch when she closes in. She's got the hots for you."

His mouth fell open. "Jenna? Not a chance."

"Just watch her. She ogles you like a lovesick puppy."

He wiped a hand across his forehead. "You never fail to surprise me."

"Don't underestimate me." She unscrewed the bottle and took a swig, enjoying the warming spirit. For the moment, it made up for the boredom of the day and the chilliness of her bedroom. She'd have to tackle that. "I don't think the bitch uses her heating. Can you switch it on?"

"Don't call her that."

Skye gave him a filthy look.

"Okay," he said. "I'll do it for you. Happy otherwise?"

She lounged back on the bed, gulping more vodka as she scrutinised her surroundings. "The view's nice, I suppose."

He brightened. "I thought you'd be impressed."

Skye rounded on him. "This flat is a dump, though. There's no TV in my room. It sucks. Can't she buy new furniture instead of this creaky old stuff?" While it was a hundred times better than many places where she'd lived, she'd moved on from that. She didn't have to put up with a slum anymore.

"It's clean and tidy," he said, adding, "We should keep it that way. There's no point in causing friction."

She continued to gripe. "And her clothes. Dated or what?"

"It's vintage. I think her dress suits her, actually."

"Actually," she mocked his snobbish accent. "Creepy charity shop gear smelling of dead people. It gives me the ick. Anyway, I warned you to keep away from her."

"I will," he promised.

"I'll go crazy staying here."

"Then do your job, and we'll get out."

Skye shook her head. "That woman is stuck up and entitled, and I'm supposed to get close to her? She winds me up."

"You can do it, sweetie," he soothed. "It's a means to an end."

"I guess so." A mellow glow spread though her as the vodka took effect. "The end justifies the means."

Skye giggled at her own cleverness. She'd learned the phrase from Douglas. As a lawyer, he often used striking language. This was a quote from Machiavelli, a rich and powerful guy who'd flourished in Renaissance Italy. Skye thought he sounded just the kind of man she'd have wished to meet if she'd lived in ancient times. Had she been born with a silver spoon in her mouth like Jenna, she could at least have gone to a posh university and learned more about him.

Douglas was an interesting person too, and a useful one. It was because of the information he'd left lying around in his office that Andrew had been able to plan this job. When she'd first begun snapping photos of documents, Skye had expected to earn a few pounds. She hadn't imagined it might lead to the kind of sum that would change her life.

Now she wasn't supposed to contact Douglas, despite ending up in Bristol thanks to him. Still, what Andrew Maxwell didn't know, wouldn't hurt him, and she deserved a little fun.

There was every reason to keep Douglas away from Jenna, though. Skye didn't trust Jenna at all.

# CHAPTER 9

## JENNA

A savoury aroma, hinting of roasted tomatoes and herbs, greeted me as I entered the flat. My stomach rumbled.

"Hello," Andrew called from the kitchen.

I hung up my coat and joined him, standing in the room's doorway once I realised Skye was hovering by the oven. The space was too narrow for three people, unless all were seated in a row at the breakfast bar. "Smells good. What's cooking?" I asked, covering my disappointment with a cheery facade. After a long day at work followed by a cash and carry trip, I'd hoped to grab a sandwich. I'd have to wait until they'd finished, though.

Skye was silent. She glanced over at the packaging strewn across the worktop.

"Oh. Pizza," I said.

"Tuesday is pizza night, right, Skye?" Andrew said. He held out a bottle of Chianti. "This'll be perfect with it. How about having a glass with me, Jenna?"

"I don't like red," Skye interrupted.

Andrew laughed. "I know, sweetie, I wasn't asking you. You don't drink at all, do you? Time enough for that when you grow up."

Her lip curled. Silently, she disposed of the food wrappings, setting out plates and cutlery for two. It was their third night in my flat, and she was already familiar with my cupboards.

"Maybe Jenna would like a slice," Andrew suggested.

Skye scowled. "There isn't enough."

"I'm not hungry," I lied.

"Have a drink," Andrew said, pouring wine into a couple of glasses. He handed one over. "Cheers. We've got something to celebrate, haven't we, Skye?"

"You mean your parking ticket?" she said to him.

"Don't you have a resident's permit yet?" I asked.

He winced. "It wasn't in Bristol," he said quickly. "And Skye knows I wasn't talking about that. No, I'm pleased to say that she's all set to start school in Bristol tomorrow. We even went out and bought all her uniform. It's a weight off my mind."

"Well done." I clinked glasses with him. "You've been busy. I guess that's why we haven't seen you in the café yet this week."

"Well, about that." Andrew's smile didn't make it to his eyes. "I'm finding your flat is a fantastic place to work. Peaceful, room to spread out—"

"Good Wi-Fi," Skye said.

"So I've gained a tenant and lost a customer."

"Your coffee will tempt me back," Andrew said. "Ah, the pizza's done."

The oven timer pinged.

"I'll see you later," I said. "Just watching the news."

I stretched out on the sofa, angling myself to see the flatscreen TV on the wall. There was talk of further interest rate rises. I emptied my wineglass.

Skye strolled past, bearing a plate with three triangles of pizza on it. My mouth watered.

She took a bite. "Going up to my room," she said. "All right?"

"Provided you don't leave crumbs." I hated myself for sounding like my stepfather.

"As if. Check the kitchen if you don't believe me."

Maybe I could make a snack now, while Andrew sat at the breakfast bar with his plate and wineglass. Scanning the worktop, I saw it was spotless. So were the utensils Skye had used.

"More wine?" he offered.

I held out my glass. "I'm impressed that you've cleaned up already."

"Skye did it. She's well-behaved."

He spoke with such pride that I was loath to contradict him. I felt guilty enough for moaning about crumbs to Skye. She and her father hardly left a trace of their existence in the kitchen. They hadn't been in the way before; apart from this evening, I'd barely seen them. In the mornings, I was up and out of the flat before they awoke.

I made a cheese toastie and took it into the living room with my drink. I'd intended to give Andrew space, but he wandered through and sat beside me.

"I am so relieved Skye's school is sorted out," he said, sipping his wine. "I'll have to work like crazy tomorrow to catch up on my projects, but at least I can relax tonight. What's on TV?"

"What do you like?"

"I'm easy. How about a comedy?" He split the rest of the bottle between our glasses.

Andrew surfed the Freeview channels until he found a cheesy sitcom. I began to mellow out, slipping into a warm fuzzy state as I pretended to watch the screen. Andrew's presence distracted me from the programme, sending a pleasant shiver across my body. I suspected he felt the same way, as we gradually inched closer to each other. His hand found mine.

I heard Skye clattering down the stairs. Quickly, I sprang away from him.

"You're disgusting."

I hadn't moved fast enough. There was no mistaking the anger in her voice.

Andrew turned around to face her. "Sweetie—"

"Don't you 'sweetie' me." She was white with rage.

"It's not what you think," I said. "The cushions are too soft. We slid into each other, that's all."

She glared at me, but I noticed her biting her lip. Perhaps I'd sown a seed of doubt.

I yawned. "I'm getting an early night." As far as I was concerned, his daughter's overreaction was Andrew's problem. I stood up, feeling her baleful eyes boring into me as I carried the empty plate and glasses to the kitchen. The pair were still hissing at each other when I returned to the living room and walked upstairs.

I'd better keep my distance unless I wanted more stress. Skye had made it clear her father was off limits.

# CHAPTER 10

## JENNA

Sam's fan club had expanded to include Skye. Although Andrew had persuaded a private school to take his daughter, presumably by signing a large cheque, she claimed to have free periods most days. After a couple of weeks, her father had settled into a routine of working in my flat, and perhaps that was why Skye dropped into the café rather than going home.

Today, she was chatting to Sam during the lunchtime lull. As I didn't serve savoury food, the café's trade petered off between twelve and two. Skye was our sole customer, if I could call her that. She'd made it clear she wouldn't buy anything.

She lounged against the counter, tiny in her school uniform. The dark blazer and plaid skirt made her look even younger. "Why do you stay in Bristol?" she asked Sam. "It's so sleepy. You could go to Hollywood."

"Hollywood hasn't come knocking at my door yet. Besides, I like Bristol. Compared to Minehead, it's a throbbing metropolis."

"I don't know Minehead." She flicked a stray blonde hair out of her eye.

"You're lucky, my love. It's a seaside resort in Somerset. Holidaymakers with hardly any money and even less sense visit it for a break. That's your geography lesson over. I'm going outside to vape."

"I'll come with you." She trotted after him. Through the window, I saw them both take vape pens from their pockets.

"Does your father know you vape?" I demanded when they returned.

Skye scowled. "Why would he care?"

From what I knew of Andrew, he would care a great deal. He only wanted the best for Skye, and had told me that morning he was off to see lawyers and apply for custody. Nothing formal had been agreed with his wife, and he feared she would go to court if he didn't begin proceedings first.

"Chill, Jenna," Sam said. "It's not like she's doing drugs."

I rounded on him. "That's exactly what she's doing. Nicotine is a drug, and whoever sold it to a fourteen-year-old is breaking the law. Andrew needs to put a stop to it."

"Well, that's between him and Skye. I'm not telling him and you shouldn't either," Sam said. "Don't pretend your parents knew everything you did as a teenager."

53

Memories surfaced of rough cider, snogging, and cigarettes. Reluctantly, I nodded. "Fair enough."

"Thanks." Skye's response was equally grudging. Her eyes swept the counter. "Got any sandwiches? I'm starving."

I winced. "No, sorry. This is a cupcake café."

"That's crazy," Skye whined. "Look how quiet it is."

"I bet there are some cake mistakes you can have," Sam said. "Isn't that right, Jenna? You baked Black Forest this morning, and half of them fall apart when you add jam."

He'd made it extraordinarily difficult for me to refuse. I arranged the broken cakes and large crumbs on a plate with a swirl of whipped cream. Remembering how Sam had entertained the customers by feeding Beth, I hoped he wouldn't be tempted to show off again. Skye, orbiting him like a planet around the sun, would have revelled in it. As Beth's friend, I felt sick at the thought. To stop a repeat performance, I handed Skye a spoon and fork.

"Enjoy."

"I shall." She tackled the sweet treat with enthusiasm.

"Great, isn't it?" Sam smiled. "Jenna is such a genius."

"Nice," Skye admitted. "Baking is your thing, Jenna, right?"

"Right. We can't all be Hollywood superstars," I said.

"I think I'd like acting. It's just pretending to be someone else, isn't it?"

"Basically," Sam said.

"What's your top tip?" Skye asked. She stretched and yawned, licking cream off her lips.

Sam copied her.

She jolted upright. "Hey, why did you do that?"

"To explain. It's not just about getting the voice right." He imitated her Birmingham accent. "You have to do the moves, too. It's harder, but once you've nailed it, the part is yours."

"So," Skye stood tall, eased herself behind the counter and pasted a grin on her face, "I am a successful entrepreneur, Miss Jenna Wyatt, with a plum in her mouth."

Her speech was a passable interpretation of mine. I reddened. A titter slipped out as I hovered between feeling flattered or insulted.

Sam took it as a sign of approval. "You've impressed Jenna," he said. "That's a good start, my love. Now walk away, go back, stand in the exact same position and do it again."

"You're kidding?" Skye pouted.

"Nope." Sam grinned. "You may need ten takes to get it right. Don't expect glamour behind the scenes."

An office worker came in and ordered cakes to take away. He didn't care about flavours, merely selecting 'pink for the girls and blue for the boys'. While I boxed them up, Skye whispered to Sam, glancing at me occasionally. I thought of a pixie and a doll, sitting in the toybox: a club of two, from which I was excluded. It was a relief when the customer left and Sam told Skye he supposed she should go back to school.

"See you later, then," she said. "You finish at five, right?"

Unable to resist interrupting, I said, "Beth will be waiting for you, surely?" Before Sam could reply to explain Beth would be toiling at the office until seven, which was always the case, I turned to Skye. "Did he explain he's taken?"

Skye's face wrinkled with scorn. "I'm not planning to hook up with him." She stalked out.

When she left, it was as if the sun had broken through clouds. My shoulders relaxed.

"You needn't fret about Skye," Sam said. "She wasn't hitting on me."

"But were you flirting with her?" I asked.

"No way." He paled. "No more than I would with anyone."

"She's trouble," I said. "Be careful."

"I will, but we ought to be kind to Skye, because she doesn't have it easy. You intimidate her. Did you realise?"

"I suppose she told you that?"

"Yes, she did."

They'd spoken about me behind my back. I stiffened again.

"Look, Jenna, cut her some slack. Skye has a psycho mother, a slimeball father and he's brought her a hundred miles to a city where she doesn't know anyone. She needs friends."

"She should make them at school." As I spoke, I was aware I sounded hypocritical. When my mother died and Richard told me he couldn't afford my boarding school fees anymore, I'd struggled at the local comprehensive in Minehead. The cool girls had made my life a misery until Sam warned them off.

He remembered. "You weren't always the best at making friends," he said gently.

"I'm just worried Skye has a crush on you."

"Like you have on her father?"

55

"Nothing's happened between us." I didn't mention Skye's uncanny knack of appearing, eyes glaring, whenever Andrew and I got too close.

"I didn't say it had yet." Sam frowned. "Keep it like that. You're on the rebound from one scumbag; you don't need another. He's too old for you, anyway."

"Not that again." My lips tightened.

"It's a pattern," he said. "When will you acknowledge it?"


# SKYE

Skye crossed the road leading to the suspension bridge, dodging traffic. She wandered past an ice-cream van parked optimistically beside the green, then took a path curving upwards through woods. School: what a joke. Whatever her plans for the afternoon, they didn't include sitting in a stuffy classroom. Despite a chilly breeze, her nostrils picked up a familiar aroma. She felt a wave of nostalgia about sharing a reefer with one of her uncles. Would the cops in Bristol care about dope smoke drifting openly in a public place? In Birmingham they didn't, as long as you didn't sit outside a police station to do it.

Maybe the Bristol fuzz were on their way. Skye didn't fancy meeting them. She continued up the slope. At its summit, an observation tower stood guard, a café tacked onto its skirts. She was no longer hungry and in no mood to buy a ticket for the observatory either. A panoramic view already lay below her, the River Avon wiggling under the majestic bridge and more of Bristol in the distance. The city sat in a basin with hills rising beyond. Nearby, the white terraces of Clifton gleamed in autumn sunshine. Past the shaggy lollipops of trees, their lush green foliage turning to russet, she spotted Jenna's house. On the top floor, her bedroom window and Jenna's stared out like a pair of eyes.

Autumn's weak sunlight lent Clifton even more sparkle. The elegance of the tall Georgian streets was the first thing Skye had noticed when Andrew brought her. Since then, she'd detected signs of wealth and comfort: the soft hum of electric cars, meek pedigree dogs being sedately walked, and an absence of betting shops. It was like a middle class theme park. She half-expected hidden speakers to belt out jolly music.

The poverty-stricken estates through which her mother moved, where sympathetic women had given Skye food and second-hand shoes until their husbands started eyeing her, could have belonged to another planet. Of course, Bristol must have council housing too. So did Minehead, by Sam's account, but Jenna's life had been sweet. She'd lived in a beautiful big house overlooking the sea.

Resentfully, Skye sucked on a pink vape bar. Jenna thought she was better than Skye, with her posh voice, pricy flat and annoyingly cute cupcake café. She had it made, with Sam doing all her work for her and Andrew paying her way too much rent. That wasn't enough, of course. Jenna might as well have had 'I heart Andrew' tattooed on her forehead. She still had the nerve to accuse Skye of chasing Sam.

Skye took it for granted that Sam would make the big time. He was a natural on screen, and not even boastful, although he'd been on Netflix. In comparison, Jenna had nothing to brag about. Anyone could bake a cake.

Sam had told Skye that he owed Jenna. It was thanks to her that he'd become an actor. Without her encouragement, he'd be working down the market like his dad, selling goods that fell off the back of a lorry. Skye didn't believe it. Sam was born to be a star, so why would his family hold him back? They sounded close-knit and happy, like hers might have been if Skye's mother wasn't off her head all the time. Drugs prised the people you loved away from you.

Sam hadn't asked about Skye's drug-addled mother and so-called father, and she'd chosen to stay quiet. Instead, she'd listened, basking in the glow of his attention. He'd told Skye to be less spiky towards Jenna. Jenna's early life had been rough. Her stepfather had been emotionally absent and her mother was dead. Their business had been sold and Jenna was forced to make her own way in the world from the age of eighteen. Surely Skye understood how hard that must be?

Skye didn't. She'd been much younger when she realised she came a poor third behind the next hit and the latest uncle. It was a while longer before she learned how to look after herself.

She'd never done a job like this before. If it had been anyone but Andrew who had suggested it, she would have said no. Sam came as an unexpected bonus, though. He was pure eye candy. Sure, he had a girlfriend and lived in Bristol, but Skye didn't plan to stay in the city for long. Why shouldn't she enjoy herself while she was here?

She caught a further whiff of marijuana and followed it down another winding path and into a small thicket. Three youths in padded jackets and jeans sat on plastic shopping bags, chatting. As she watched, holding her breath, they passed a blunt between them.

They looked up at her approach, eyeing the frumpy school uniform. Although she'd crept towards them, the undergrowth was dense and dry. It was impossible not to make a noise. That would alert the group if the police turned up too, she supposed.

"Hey, kid." One of them met her eyes. He was tall and rangy, with dark curly hair, probably about her age.

"Can I share?" She displayed her sweetest smile.

He laughed, not unkindly. "No. Go home and play with your dolls."

"Or play with yourself." The second boy sniggered, his leer a slash in a mess of acne.

Skye didn't bother to spare him a glance. She focused on the leader. Removing her backpack, she unzipped it to reveal a bottle of vodka. "I have a better idea," she said. "Swapsies?"

# CHAPTER 11

## A MAN WITH A PROBLEM

His plans for this October morning hadn't included a trip to the middle of nowhere, but when Sheila Vincent told you to jump, you didn't ask questions. He'd rearranged his diary and set off. Why she lived in the dreary Worcestershire countryside was beyond him. Her wealth would buy a flat in any city in the world. Still, he'd raid the library on his visit. That would ensure it wasn't a waste of time.

He stopped for coffee at a service station on the M5. Hearing his phone buzz as he returned to the car, he set down his takeaway cup to look. McPherson had sent a message: a video without a caption.

His throat constricted. The desire for caffeine vanished. He had been juggling creditors and dropped a ball; the instalment due to McPherson yesterday hadn't been paid. With mounting dread, he pressed play, knowing it wouldn't be a jokey cartoon.

The short clip showed a horse, a fine white thoroughbred, jumping over a fence. The animal's feet didn't clear the obstacle. It fell, throwing its rider. Whinnying, the poor beast struggled and failed to get up. Then a man, face obscured by his windcheater, approached with a captive bolt pistol. He fired into the head at point blank range. The horse's desperate thrashing ceased.

He made it back inside to a toilet cubicle before he was sick. As if the gist wasn't clear enough, a short text arrived from McPherson: 'Such a shame.'

It was a few minutes before he'd stopped retching and calmed down enough to drive away. Even then, he almost hit another vehicle as he reversed from his parking space.

The motorway was busy when he rejoined it. That helped. He couldn't chew over his problems while he concentrated on traffic. Later, in the quiet country lanes near Bruntney, he wondered if he should have replied to McPherson straight away. Better to wait until he had the cash, he decided. That shouldn't be long if he stuffed a few rare volumes in his laptop case.

He didn't notice the black car until he drove on a long straight stretch of road. It appeared in his rearview mirror, gradually gaining on him but never catching up. If he hadn't received those missives from McPherson, he'd have thought no more about it. A chill ran down his spine. He braked sharply, taking a corner at the last minute without indicating. It wasn't the route he'd intended, but it would still bring him to Bruntney Manor.

His shadow followed. Heart racing, he tried speeding up, slowing down, accelerating again and swivelling quickly around corners. It was impossible to shake off the black car, and he no longer had doubts. Could he get away? His first panicked instinct was to flee, but the other driver was too good. Only a madman would continue to the manor and bring a thug to Sheila's doorstep. A showdown was his only option.

He was in a single-track, rutted lane, rarely used. Cuttings had been made at intervals to widen the road and provide a passing place. In one of these, he brought his car to a halt. Trees, brown and almost leafless, rose up on either side. No-one could see the lane from the fields beyond. That suited him. Reaching in his pocket, he felt the cold, smooth metal of a Swiss Army knife. He'd have the element of surprise. In spite of his fear, he was energised, his face flushed with excitement.

The tail, a Honda Accord, overtook him and parked in front, blocking the road in that direction. Minutes ticked by. Nothing happened. He clutched the knife, breathing heavily, unwilling to show his hand first. When would his opponent make a move? Finally, his phone vibrated with another message from McPherson: 'Get out of the car.'

He was damned whatever he did. McPherson's man might petrol-bomb his vehicle if he stayed inside. Yet out in the open, he'd be a target if the Honda was used as a weapon. Defying McPherson was probably the worst of the two evils. He leaped out, leaving his door open and scuttling behind the car. At least it would act as a shield.

Two figures in black hoodies, masks stretched across their faces, emerged from the Honda. When he saw the pistol, he realised the knife would be no use.

Hyperventilating, he forced his lips into what he hoped was a friendly smile. "How can I help?"

"Cut the crap. We haven't got long." The man with the gun wasn't a Londoner like McPherson; he had a local accent. It explained how he knew the roads.

"You're coming with us," his companion said.

If he obeyed, he wouldn't bet on living to a ripe old age. "I'm getting the money," he croaked. "I have a lady friend—"

"Is that so?" The gunman sounded amused.

"—and she's going to help me out."

"A bit late, isn't it?"

"I know. I'm sorry."

"Well," the gunman drawled, bringing his weapon only inches away, "Mr McPherson would say sorry isn't enough."

The gun was pressed against his forehead now in a sickening echo of the video. He didn't soil himself, but it was close. A cold sweat drenched him. Voice shaking, he rasped, "What would McPherson rather have? Money or revenge?"

The gunman snorted. "Both, I'd say." With a swift movement, he swung the gun downwards, smashing it towards the crotch.

Pain exploded. His legs gave way and he fell to his knees, screaming as soon as he caught his breath again. The agony consumed him. His vision swimming, he didn't see his assailants return to their car. He barely heard their parting threat either.

"Tell her you've got a headache," the gunman said. "I'd pay up if I were you. Next time, Mr McPherson will tell me to press the trigger. And it's more than my life's worth to refuse."

# CHAPTER 12

## JENNA

After Skye had moaned once again about the lack of lunch items, I'd trialled a range of savoury muffins. To my surprise, they'd done well. The café was still losing money, though. At the end of October, I decided to close on Mondays and Tuesdays, the quietest part of the week. I was running a business. While I loved my customers, I'd never planned on paying them to turn up, and I was effectively doing that.

It came as a relief to stay in bed late for a change. I also looked forward to seeing Andrew, although not without trepidation. I'd had enough of Skye's backchat, and once she'd gone to school, I'd tell him. We sometimes watched TV together in the evenings, but I couldn't speak privately with him when a scowling Skye might appear at any moment.

Protective father that he was, I suspected he wouldn't believe that she was anything other than perfect. I must be as tactful as possible, because I also had to tackle him about his rent. He'd agreed to pay weekly in advance. At first, he'd brought credit cards to the café every Sunday, but I'd had nothing from him this week.

I was less than thrilled to find Skye alone in the living room on Tuesday morning. "Where's your father? And why aren't you at school?"

"Dad went off on business. He wanted to see you before he left, but you were asleep. Anyway, he'll be back by the weekend."

It was annoying that Andrew had left without telling me, but worse to be treated like an unpaid babysitter. I added it to my mental checklist of points to discuss.

Skye fingered the TV remote. "I've got a free period, but there's nothing to watch on here. I'll try Netflix."

"I never had so much time off school."

She shrugged. "Those were the old days."

"Not that long ago. I'm twenty-six."

The ghost of a sneer flitted across her face. I checked myself. Skye was fourteen, almost half my age. I must seem ancient to her. She was right to point out that life had changed, too. The pandemic had disrupted classes. Clearly, she'd been working: a black plastic folder labelled 'GEOG' lay on the coffee table. She wore her uniform and must intend to go into school later. Until then, I'd have to pander to her whims. My heart sank.

Skye picked up on my discomfort. "Don't blame me if Dad didn't say anything," she griped. "Anyhow, why should he? You're his landlady, not his lover."

I gawped at her. "He shouldn't have left you by yourself."

She shrugged. "I don't see why not. Anyway, he hasn't, has he? You're here."

That was the point. On the verge of hiding in my bedroom to phone him, I decided to wait until after breakfast. I padded to the kitchen.

Skye followed me. "Can we have bacon and eggs?" she whined.

"Feel free to make it."

"I will. With mushrooms. You can have some too."

"Yes please." Curious at this rare outburst of generosity, I made a cup of instant coffee and sat down to watch her at work.

It was the first time I'd spent more than a minute alone with Skye, or seen her cook from scratch. Andrew and his daughter usually microwaved ready meals in the evening. There was no more home-made boeuf bourguignon from Andrew, and I suspected it had really come from a supermarket. Skye always took food to her room, while Andrew sat in the kitchen to eat, often joining me later as I lounged in front of the TV.

Skye knew the location of my pans and utensils. From Andrew's section of the fridge, she produced eggs, button mushrooms and butter. AirPods in her ears, she set the mushrooms sizzling in a pan, then returned to the fridge for bacon.

"That's mine," I protested.

"What?" She removed her AirPods.

"I bought that streaky to make supper tonight. Look, it's from Aldi. Andrew doesn't go there."

"But we're sharing," she carped.

"Never mind." It wasn't worth the battle, especially when I recalled student flat share feuds. They always began with vanishing rashers.

Skye added the remaining ingredients. They bubbled and sputtered. A delicious aroma filled the room and my mouth watered. This was so different from my typical start to the day, a bowl of microwaved porridge. I couldn't wait to tuck in.

"You can have half, all right?" she said, placing two plates on the worktop.

"Thanks. It smells great."

After I'd complimented her on the tasty meal, we ate together silently, Skye's movements dainty as she cut her food into pieces. I was reminded again of a porcelain doll.

She finished her last mouthful and stretched. "Got geography homework. Can you help me?"

"I'll try, but it's years since I did any."

"This will be easy for you, I bet. Can I take a photo of your passport?"

It seemed an odd request. "How does that fit with your homework project? Anyway, don't you have your own?"

Skye shrugged. "The teacher said we had to do it, and I don't know where mine is. Dad takes care of all that. Please, Jenna. It's my first lesson."

"All right." Although tempted to say she shouldn't leave her homework to the last minute, I took the line of least resistance.

Skye followed me into the living room, observing me as I removed my passport from the desk where I kept important documents. I handed it to her.

"Thanks." She snapped the photo page with her phone. "Got to lie down before going out. I feel sick."

My stomach lurched as I recalled earlier fears about Skye sprinkling my food with arsenic. Fortunately, the sensation passed. Seized by a burst of energy, I washed up the breakfast things, then brought my sewing machine to the kitchen table. Humming along to Miley Cyrus, I made glittery bunting for Christmas. The decorations wouldn't go up for a couple of months, but I liked to plan ahead.

The front door slammed. As usual, Skye hadn't said goodbye. I tutted, but I was relieved to be alone again. Finishing the bunting, I switched on the TV. My gaze was drawn to the A4 folder on the coffee table. Skye had left her geography coursework behind.

I didn't have her number, Even if I had, a text might disrupt a lesson. Her school lay only a ten-minute walk away, though, so why not take the notes to her?

I threw on my polka dot mac, grabbed the bag and folder, and hurried out into the chilly air. A sharp wind stung my cheeks as I walked across Christchurch Green. The park separated Clifton Village's shops and bars from a residential area beyond. Behind the stone houses lay two private schools and a zoo, all centuries old. The distant roar of lions competed with birdsong nearby. While the zoo had recently closed, not all the animals had been shipped out yet. Many would leave soon for roomier premises on the city's outskirts.

I wondered what my future held. The green spaces, bars, and coffee culture were the reasons I'd settled in Clifton. I'd enjoyed them at weekends when I worked in insurance, but I never had time or money nowadays. Still, Andrew's rent helped, at least when I received it. What would I do when he and his daughter moved out?

Her school occupied extensive grounds on the other side of the green. Its buildings were a mix of mellow stone mansions and twentieth century infill. Hedges, walls, and railings, sometimes all three, protected its boundaries. Skirting the perimeter, I found an imposing, black-railed gate. It was locked. A keypad beside it obviously gave entry to those who knew the code.

I pressed the buzzer underneath.

With a crackle of static, a woman's voice said, "Good morning." She sounded refined and middle-aged. I felt a pang of sympathy for Skye; with her Birmingham accent, she probably struggled to fit in.

"I've brought a geography folder for Skye Maxwell," I said.

"Are you a parent?" her genteel tones demanded.

"No." Put on the spot, I didn't give the best description of our relationship. "I, er, share a flat with her father."

"I see. I don't recognise the pupil's name, I'm afraid. Can you spell it, please?"

"S-K-Y-E..." I finished by lamely explaining that she was new.

"Bear with me." There was a long silence, then she said, "I'm having difficulty tracing her. Are you sure she's a pupil here?"

"Um, maybe not. Sorry."

Having made excuses, I tried another private school, which boasted an even grander campus nearby. Skye Maxwell was a stranger there, too. This school was divided into houses, and it didn't help that Skye had never spoken of one or mentioned her teachers' names. I returned home with her folder, bracing myself for a tantrum when she found out I had it.

The afternoon passed in a whirl of craft projects. I mended a skirt, then found oddments of pastel-coloured wool, perfect for tea cosies. Sitting on the sofa with a cuppa, knitting as daylight faded beyond the suspension bridge, I'd almost forgotten about Skye.

The key turned in the lock. She marched through the front door and headed towards the staircase.

"Skye, you left your geography project behind."

"No worries. I had what I needed," she called behind her.

"I took the folder to your school. They claimed they had no record of you."

That grabbed her attention. She turned around. "Why did you interfere? I told you I didn't need it."

I blinked. "I didn't know that earlier. You seemed stressed about your homework this morning. Anyway, why would they say there was no pupil called Skye Maxwell?"

Skye blushed, tension visible in her stance. She folded her arms. "I suppose he told you he was married to my mum?"

I saw where this was going. "Yes."

"Well, he isn't. I don't have his surname."

"So what—"

"It doesn't matter. Why should I tell you? You'll only embarrass me again."

"Skye, it's nothing to be ashamed of—"

Huffing, she stomped up to her room before I could open up to her. At least she had a father who thought the world of her, and she knew who he was. Mine could be anybody apart from Richard. What was the point of guessing at his identity? If he cared about me, he'd have found me by now.

I wiped away a tear before picking up a stitch that had slipped off the needle. Giving the knitting my full attention again, I tried to forget.

Twenty minutes later, Skye reappeared, heels click-clacking down the stairs. She wore stilettos, thick make-up and little else. Her strappy top and pelmet skirt were the sort of clothes my friends and I had chosen when we went clubbing as students. We'd been eighteen when we teetered down Park Street, barhopping. Skye was four years our junior: far too young.

I took a deep breath, preparing for the inevitable confrontation. "Skye, where are you going?"

She glared. "What's it to you?"

How I wished Andrew was here. His daughter couldn't be trusted to stay out of trouble. While he shouldn't have left her in my care, he'd never forgive me if Skye ended up blind-drunk or worse. I wouldn't forgive myself either.

"Skye, you can't go out looking like that and expect me not to worry about you. I'm phoning your dad."

"Why? I'm only seeing a friend. We're doing our homework together." A calculating expression stole across her face. "All right. I'll get changed."

# SKYE

"Where are your books? And your laptop?"

"I don't need them." Skye marched out of the flat. Would Jenna never stop bleating? Having wiped off cosmetics and put her school uniform on again, she was in no mood to back down further. It wasn't even necessary to roleplay a stroppy adolescent. Jenna's high-handed manner pushed all her buttons.

A taxi whisked her to Douglas's hotel in the centre of Bristol. This was a Victorian building decorated in a modern style. He sat in the lobby on a scarlet egg-shaped chair, Lobb-clad feet parked on a swirly rug. The environment suited him. Poor Douglas imagined himself a snappy dresser, with his flamboyant silk ties and artfully curled hair. Really, he was just an old man trying too hard.

Douglas rose to greet her, a light kiss on each cheek. There would be no snogging in public; they were both too careful for that. He clasped her hands. "I've missed you, baby," he whispered.

"Me too," she lied.

"I thought you were in Bristol on holiday. Why the school uniform?"

She stuck out her lower lip. "Don't you like it?"

"I do, very much. Sadly, they won't let you in my favourite cocktail lounge. I told you I knew a place, didn't I?"

That was typical of Douglas. You could name any city and he'd find a high-end bar. He was generous with his credit card, too.

"Sorry about that." She suppressed her annoyance with Jenna. Nothing would stop her having a ball, even if it was just in Douglas's bedroom. Taking a step back, she regarded him through lowered lashes. "What's in your minibar?"

# CHAPTER 13

## JENNA

I was exhausted. Skye hadn't returned from 'doing homework' until 2am. There was no sign of an apology. While her breath stank of alcohol, she didn't appear to be a merry drunk. Her mood was as foul as ever. She hissed with outrage when I told her I'd phoned Andrew. He'd been distraught, but didn't want me to report her as missing for fear he'd lose custody. I hadn't even managed to get Skye's full name from him, just a promise to return to Bristol to search for her.

He'd evidently cancelled that plan once I'd texted to say she was safe. When my alarm clock woke me at six, I'd soon established he wasn't back. The open boxroom door had revealed his duvet neatly folded on the mattress. There was no laptop on the desk. Bleary-eyed, I'd staggered around the flat, little caring if my clumsy noisiness disturbed Skye. Since then, I'd dragged myself through a day of brain fog. It was a miracle I'd only dropped one tray of cakes and made mistakes with two orders.

Andrew was losing his charm for me. He came with too much baggage in the form of an impossible teenager. If only I could manage without his money. Having said that, he still owed me rent, and I phoned him at lunchtime to ask for it. He didn't pick up. I decided to play hardball, texting a warning that the pair would have to move out if he didn't pay.

After gently prising the story out of me, Sam offered to mediate with Skye. However, she didn't show her face in the café all day. Dreading another confrontation with her, I closed up at the end of a long shift. My feet felt like dead weights as I climbed the stairs to my flat.

About to unlock the door, I stopped. Andrew's voice could clearly be heard. Despite listening intently, I couldn't make out his words, nor Skye's answering whine.

Hairs prickled on the back of my neck. This was a side to Andrew I'd never seen: the angry father rather than the caring one. His tone was steely, while Skye wheedled. She clearly hoped to calm him down, but it was no use. His fury escalated. "You have no idea what she wants," he yelled.

Skye began to cry.

I fiddled with my fingers, standing back from the door. I suspected whatever the reason for Andrew's criticism, Skye deserved it. He was probably giving her a hard time about last night. Still, I didn't want to be caught eavesdropping. Waiting until Skye's sobs subsided, I stamped my feet on the landing and ground my key in the lock.

Andrew sat alone on the sofa, contemplating the suspension bridge with its flow of rush hour traffic.

"You're back," I said. "Thank goodness. I was so concerned about Skye."

He angled his face toward me, grinning, his posture relaxed. There was no indication he'd just had a blazing row.

"Girls will be girls," he said, rolling his eyes.

"I thought I heard her cry?"

He grimaced. "Yes, I'm sorry, Jenna. I told Skye I expected better behaviour from her. She can be over-sensitive, but it's natural after all she's been through. Best to leave her be."

I nodded. The less I interacted with Skye, the better. Once he handed over the cash he owed, I would tell him not to disappear overnight without her again. "Did you get my text about the rent?" I asked.

"Yes." He sat upright, feet twisted together. "I hesitated to mention it, because I was shocked by your heartless threat. I've been out of my mind with worry for my daughter."

"I was anxious about her too." Guilt gnawed at my stomach. I needed the cash, though: enough to tell a white lie. "Andrew, a friend asked me today if they could rent your two rooms. Obviously, you know my financial situation. I was tempted, I'm afraid, especially as I hate having to badger you. Could you set up a direct debit to save embarrassment in future?"

"I'll come into the café tomorrow and pay by card." Andrew stood, stretching. "Sorry, a client is taking me out to dinner. Must dash."

I wished him a pleasant evening. My limbs felt leaden, drained of energy. Making my way to the kitchen, I reached for the half-full bottle of Pinot Grigio in the fridge. There was less wine than I thought, so I tipped the lot into a glass. Skye might have helped herself to a drink earlier, but I was past caring. After the last twenty-four hours, I needed to unwind.

The flat was comfortably warm now I could afford to heat it. I dozed off watching TV, jolting awake an hour later and stumbling into bed without supper.

The next morning, energy levels restored, I zipped around the flat to gather rubbish and recycling. A collection was due later, and I didn't want to miss it. Had I been less shattered, I'd have carried out the task before going to bed.

A flash of blue caught my eye as I emptied the bathroom bin. To my horror, I realised it was the packaging for a pregnancy test.

It could only belong to Skye. My throat constricted. I'd had suspicions about risky behaviour, but this was worse than I thought. She was a child of fourteen and deserved to be treated like one, yet somebody had taken advantage of her.

The little box was torn at one end. Here, the test stick had been shoved back in. Its tip poked out, taunting me to look. When I did, the blue plus sign confirmed my fears. Skye was pregnant.

Her father needed to be told, but shouldn't I speak to her first? Heart pounding, I glanced at her bedroom door. It remained firmly shut, no sound emerging from within. I'd just have to hope she visited the café today before Andrew. It would be awkward otherwise. He'd agreed to come by today, and I'd have trouble looking him in the eye without spilling Skye's secret.

First, I had to console Sam, late for work this morning because his bicycle had been stolen. He'd had to hire an e-scooter.

"I didn't think anyone would nick the old boneshaker," he said.

"Maybe they took a shine to your flowers," I suggested. He'd painted daisies all over the metalwork for a charity bike ride. The effect harmonised perfectly with my café's style, so I'd begged him to keep it that way. It had suited Sam to park up right outside, too.

Sam's spirits lifted when I presented him with a Black Forest cupcake, his favourite. "I guess in Bristol, you only rent a bicycle," he admitted. We agreed that if he spotted a bargain in the small ads, I'd give him time off to chase it.

I started baking the lunchtime muffins. As if on cue, Skye slipped into the café. She made a beeline for Sam.

"Hello stranger." He smiled at her. "These courgette muffins are selling like hot cakes. Want one?"

"I'm not hungry." Her eyes darted here and there. "Are you on your break yet? I need a vape."

"Sam's busy," I said. "I'll come outside with you." I grabbed my coat before Sam contradicted me.

Outside it was quiet, our sole audience the windows of mews houses opposite. I shivered in the damp autumn air. Although the heaviest garment Skye wore was a blazer, she seemed unaffected.

She didn't look at me. Fiddling with a pocket on her backpack, she removed a crimson disposable vape bar and sucked on its mouthpiece. Seconds later, she blew out a plume of sickly sweet smoke.

I stifled a cough. "What flavour is it?" I asked.

"Cherry berry."

"Are you still feeling sick?" If she was, her vape bar wouldn't help. As I inhaled its scent, nausea wormed its way up my throat.

Her gaze was focused ahead of her. "I'm okay. Not hungry, that's all."

My heart thumped. This was my chance to broach the subject with her, but how? She was like a frightened animal, inclined to lash out when unsettled.

"Skye?" I kept my voice low, my tone friendly. "I saw your pregnancy test."

I'd believed she might deny it, but she said nothing at all.

"Does Andr – does your father know?"

"What do you think?" She made no attempt to conceal her scorn.

"He'll be sympathetic, I'm sure. It must be a big shock for him. And you."

I wished she would give me eye contact. Instead, she vaped furiously, enveloping me in a synthetic-smelling cloud.

"Look, Skye, you need to tell the boy. If you don't want to, I can talk to him or his parents. Was it the friend you saw on Tuesday?"

"Stay out of it."

"Skye, the problem won't go away. We have to deal with it—"

She rounded on me. At last, I could see her eyes. They were hostile. "What do you mean, we? I'm handling it, all right?"

I stared at her. "You're fourteen. You need help with this. And the police may have to get involved. You're underage, for God's sake." I was aware that I sounded shrill. While I couldn't imagine Skye was ready to be a mother, neither was I. Andrew had thrust responsibility for Skye onto me, and I was struggling to cope.

"Are you real?" she demanded. "I've had sex. Big deal. And you can talk. Sam says in Minehead, they're hardly out of the cradle when they start. My dad doesn't want you to speak to the police, and nor do I."

I swallowed, determined to stay positive. A little girl lost lay behind the bravado and barbed comments. I must remember that. "If you're sure," I said. "If I'm right, he's cross, isn't he? I'll do my best to calm him down when I see him later."

"You'll be lucky," Skye sneered. "He's out doing business again."

There would be no rent for me today, then. How had Andrew forgotten so easily? Lips pressed tight, I considered the possibility that he didn't intend to pay. I shuddered.

"Cold?" Skye asked stonily.

I switched my focus back to her. "You have my support, Skye. I can go with you to the doctor, or talk to the baby's father for you, for instance. Whatever you need."

"What I need is for you to back off." Skye took a long drag. "There won't be a baby, all right? I'm getting rid of it, so it doesn't matter who the father is." Tucking the vape bar into her backpack again, she stalked away.

# CHAPTER 14

## SKYE

She'd had the abortion. All it took was a few pills, and a day in bed guzzling vodka and chocolates to get over the cramps. You didn't even need to see a doctor. If it had been this easy twenty years ago, she probably wouldn't exist. Skye's mother had often moaned to friends about her trouble in seeking a termination. Did she think Skye wouldn't hear about it?

Like her mother, Skye wasn't one hundred per cent certain of the father's identity, but she could make a good guess. Jenna would have freaked out if she'd realised. The woman was beyond stupid: she didn't see what was happening right under her nose.

Obviously, she hadn't told Jenna that the deed was done. It suited Skye for her landlady to believe in the pregnancy. That way, Skye wouldn't be thrown out on the streets. Andrew had been away for a week and he owed rent. He took too many risks. After all, they needed to live here, so why wouldn't he pay? She'd have to do it herself if Jenna turned nasty and told them to leave. In a bored moment, Skye had set up a fake dating profile, requesting donations to a cash app 'if you're serious'. Her bank balance was healthy. Suppose she did give Jenna the cash, though? There would be awkward questions. Who wanted the hassle?

Now Skye was taking it easy. She'd ordered a late lunch from Domino's and poured herself a glass from the bottle of white wine that Jenna kept in the fridge. Jenna never noticed how quickly it disappeared. Lounging on the sofa, Skye surfed the web on her phone, browsing Grace Vincent's new collection. There was a short gold dress that would look amazing on her. Skye imagined wearing it to a film premiere with Sam. She would glide across the red carpet, attracting admiration and envy in equal measure. TV cameras would be all over her, the beautiful girl in the latest Grace Vincent.

Skye followed Grace on social media. She liked Grace's bright, upbeat posts and images of sexy clothes in exotic locations. Not only that, but Sam actually knew Grace, and Skye had picked up pieces of gossip. Sam had met Grace on a film. He raved about her authenticity. There was a connection through Douglas too; he'd been friends with Grace's father. Perhaps he'd get her a discount on the dress. If Skye was sweet to him, he might even buy it.

She'd pay him in kind, of course, maintaining the fiction that she found her sugar daddy irresistible. At least Douglas was fit. He kept his body lean and muscled with gym workouts and mountain climbing. When she lay back and closed her eyes, his grey hair vanished and she imagined a much younger man. Last time, Sam had been the object of her fantasy. Skye grinned at the memory.

A buzzer signalled the arrival of a visitor. It must be the pizza. Skye pressed a button to open the front door on the ground floor.

"Come on up."

A man's voice spoke through the intercom instead. "I've got a letter for Miss Jenna Wyatt. Signed delivery."

"I'll take it."

The postman made it clear she should go downstairs for it. Sighing, Skye left the flat to meet him.

"Jenna Wyatt?" he asked.

"Yes."

He didn't bat an eyelid. Either it wasn't his regular round, or he didn't care who took the embossed cream envelope. He didn't request a signature either; since the pandemic, no-one bothered with that.

Skye felt the smooth paper and the raised Millican Syme crest on the flap. Her glee bubbled over. She danced back to the flat, knocking back her wine and refilling the glass. "Cheers," she announced to the empty room, before sending Andrew a text: 'letter here xoxoxo'.

He phoned her straight back. "Have you opened it?"

"I'll do it right now."

The familiar Millican Syme logo jumped out at her. She read the letter out to him.

Andrew chuckled. "We're in business, sweetie."

"So what next?"

"Need you ask? You reply to Millican Syme so we can finish the job. Oh, and I'll arrange a meeting with Douglas Millican in Edinburgh."

"Edinburgh?" Skye wrinkled her face. "Why are you seeing him there? He's based in Birmingham."

"Damn straight, sweetie. But Douglas Millican knows you. When you visit Millican Syme, I want him as far away as possible."

"Right." Skye looked out of the window, watching seagulls fly over the bridge. Soon she would be free and happy like them. "I want to get out of here. When are we leaving?"

"Got somewhere to stay then, have you?"

"You're not offering?" she asked.

"I've found another mark. You'd cramp my style, sweetie. Sorry."

"I'll get an Airbnb in Brum." Returning to Birmingham made sense. Millican Syme were based there. She could have rented a studio in Bristol like Andrew had, before they took these rooms, but she wanted to steer clear of Jenna.

"I'm returning to Bristol to whisk you away. Get packed, sweetie. Don't forget the essentials we talked about. Mwah."

She reciprocated with a mock kiss, skipping around the room when he'd cut the call. Although she'd miss Sam, she couldn't wait to escape from Jenna's suffocating presence. After a celebratory swig of wine, she collected the items Andrew had asked for.

# JENNA

A fine spray of rain, at that intermediate stage between mist and drizzle, coated my hair. My feet ached as I limped home from the café, looking forward to kicking off my shoes. It had been a long day without Sam, called away to an audition in London. Naturally, I'd struggled solo to save on the wage bill. Temporary staff were a luxury I couldn't afford. The café was getting busier at last, though. Skye's insistence on lunchtime snacks had made a real difference.

While grateful for that, I still had mixed feelings about Skye. She'd avoided me since I'd spoken to her about the baby. When our paths crossed, perhaps as she passed through the living room to make tea in the kitchen, she was subdued rather than aggressive. I occasionally heard her throw up in the bathroom. She couldn't have terminated the pregnancy yet, but I didn't risk a row by asking. She was the least of my worries now. Andrew had left on another business trip. He'd stacked up a fortnight of rent arrears, and Skye pleaded ignorance of his whereabouts.

As I approached my home, I saw no light in the windows of the upper floors. I supposed Skye was out with one of her friends. Hopefully, she wouldn't be back late. Now Andrew was ignoring calls and texts, I'd have no way of alerting him if she indulged in risky behaviour again. Sighing, I trudged upstairs, opening the door to the flat and flicking on the living room switch.

Andrew and Skye usually tidied up after themselves. I'd even caught her cleaning the bathroom. On this point, at least, I'd had no complaints about her. Yet now, an empty wine glass stood on the coffee table. Beside it, a cardboard pizza box lay open, revealing crumbs and a few half-chewed crusts. The sweet scent of Skye's favourite vape bar suffused the air.

She'd been drinking my wine after all. Not just that, but she'd been vaping inside my flat. It was unacceptable, and I'd have to tell her. There was no way of avoiding a conflict with her now.

I checked the kitchen and tried the lavatory door, knowing as soon as it opened that she wasn't inside. Dashing upstairs, my exasperation turned to concern. Skye shouldn't be touching alcohol and nicotine in her condition. Surely she'd learned that at school? I remembered PSHE lessons where the mean girls had done their best to embarrass our teachers. It was typical of Skye, too, to brush off those in authority. Knowing her, she wouldn't have bothered visiting a doctor after taking her home pregnancy test. Andrew might not even have registered her with a GP in Bristol. He was a doting father but not, I'd realised, a diligent one.

A worse possibility crossed my mind. Suppose Skye had suffered a miscarriage? If so, I should cut her some slack. I shivered, imagining Skye all alone, wracked with pain and blood. "Skye?" I called, my voice gentle. Tentatively, I knocked on the door to her room and pushed it open.

It was empty. Not only was Skye absent, but so were her possessions: the two huge pink suitcases and the vast array of clothes and toiletries that had emerged from them when she moved in. I checked the wardrobe, an old pine piece which I'd lovingly stencilled with tulips. There was no sign she'd ever used it. The bathroom's bare shelves told a similar story. Skye's rose-scented shower gel and Andrew's Imperial Leather no longer hung from the shower rail.

Andrew's boxroom was also devoid of his things. On the desk, however, he'd left a scribbled note: 'Skye ran away. I'm worried. Will bring her back when I find her.'

There was no mention of rent. Why would there be when he was overwhelmed with concern for Skye? Yet Andrew wouldn't have taken all his belongings if he'd intended to return. My breath quickened. I tried to slow it and quell the knot in my stomach. Picking up my phone, I found Andrew's number.

The call went to voicemail. I left a message and followed up with a text, but I didn't expect a reply. Andrew's actions spoke louder than words. He'd done a stealth move, and that was the last I'd see of him or his rent.

# CHAPTER 15

## SKYE

It was an Airbnb flat similar to others where Skye had stayed: upmarket and bland. Invariably they were decorated in white or cream, with kitchen units built into the lounge to maximise space for bedrooms. Floors and furniture were light wood, easy to wipe clean. Modern prints in matching frames dotted the walls.

She made a habit of renting such places for a week at a time, moving around the wealthier parts of Birmingham's city centre and its suburbs. She preferred apartment blocks, where people often came and went. No-one would notice or comment on the number and type of her visitors. Anonymity brought risks, though, especially unwelcome callers. A girl on her own was an easy target for extortion. For that reason, she didn't stay anywhere long.

Andrew knew the score. In the past, he'd visited several of her lodgings as a paying client. She was too professional to mention names, but she had let slip that she frequently visited a lawyer's office. Andrew had spotted the potential immediately. At first, he'd given her cash for gossip, then a further amount when she snapped pictures of documents on display in Douglas's office. That was when Andrew found out about Mitch Vincent's estate. It changed everything.

They were equal partners now. She just wished he'd remember. Yet while he cultivated a mark, a rich widow, he expected Skye to stay closeted away like a nun. She supposed she could have dressed like one. For Douglas's visit, however, she had chosen the ugly school uniform.

What was the harm in seeing Douglas? She was bored with drinking and watching Netflix. It was too risky to show up at his office anymore, she understood that, but an assignation in this flat held no dangers. You were here today, gone tomorrow. It might be the last time she met him. She'd miss Douglas. He had become more than a lucrative side hustle, she realised: he'd given her a window to another world.

A bell sounded as she lounged on the ubiquitous leather sofa, fourth can of vodka and tonic in hand. Sighing, she rose, and buzzed Douglas in.

"Nice outfit, baby."

"Thanks."

He kissed her hungrily, then scanned the room, eyes drawn to the French doors at one end. This was the apartment's USP: a balcony overlooking a canal and identical properties on the far side of the water.

"You're doing well for yourself," he said.

She didn't bother to explain. "Want a drink?" She'd bought a couple of whisky miniatures for him, a brand she'd seen in his office.

"Just the one. I can't stay long. I've got to prepare for a trip to Edinburgh. Would you like to come with me? My hotel has an excellent cocktail bar."

Skye pretended to consider it. "Sorry, not this time."

"Scotland too far for you? I know it's another country, but you don't need a passport."

She had a passport; it just wasn't her own. "I'll make that drink," she said, gesturing to the sofa.

He took the hint and sat down while she found ice cubes in the freezer compartment. Adding them to a glass, she splashed in a measure of Glenfiddich.

"Cheers." She handed him the whisky and snuggled beside him, relaxing as he stroked her neck.

Douglas removed her school tie and began undoing the buttons of her blouse, his breathing heavy.

Skye wriggled away. He enjoyed the thrill of the chase, so she shouldn't make it easy for him. "Douglas?" she asked.

"Yes, baby?"

"If I came into some money, where's the best place to stash it?"

He sat bolt upright. "You cannot be serious, Skye. What have you got yourself mixed up in?"

"Nothing," she muttered. "Sorry." It had been the vodka talking. She wished she hadn't said anything. Still, how would Douglas possibly guess her plans?

Douglas exhaled. "If you are in some sort of trouble, get your funds into a foreign bank account. Somewhere like Panama, where the cost of living is cheap and the law can't touch you. That's my best advice."

"Thanks." Skye stood up. She parted her lips, licking them with the tip of her tongue, desperate to flee towards safer ground. "How about bed?"

Douglas slapped her rump. "Now you're talking," he leered.

That was how it had begun. It was how it always ended.

"So, sweetie, who's the first person you'll see in the building?"

"There's a man sitting at a desk. A dude in a suit during the day, then an old security guard at night."

"And what do you say to him?" Andrew demanded.

Skye bit back a sarcastic retort. She stared at the window, its canalside view hidden by streaks of rain. November in Birmingham: she was living the dream. "Ha," she said. "I know better than to let on I've seen him before. It's 'Good morning, I have an appointment with Millican Syme'."

"Suppose he asks who you're meeting there? And lose that Brummie accent, will you? It isn't Meelykin Soy-im."

She coloured. "What's wrong with it? I'm proud to come from Birmingham. Aren't you, then?"

"Yes, but that's not what they'll be expecting. You're supposed to have gone to a private school, like the one in Bristol whose doors you never actually darkened. Go on, say it again."

"Millican Syme." Skye yawned. "Do we have to do this? I want a drink. When you asked yourself round to roleplay, I figured you meant something else."

He eyed her lasciviously. "There's a thought, sweetie. Still got that school uniform?"

"No." She'd taken the awful garments to a storage unit she rented in north Birmingham, to which she'd also returned the bubblegum-pink suitcases. Special outfits and a selection of toys were neatly arranged there too. When she desired a change, she'd take a cab. Perhaps she should have waited before banishing the uniform, though. What was it with old men and schoolgirls? Guys were so predictable.

"Never mind," Andrew said. "Listen, you shouldn't drink before tomorrow, okay? You'll be giving the performance of your life. But if you fancy stopping for a line of coke, be my guest." He flung a few twists of paper on the kitchen counter.

She eyed them greedily. "Is that all you've got?"

Andrew sighed, fishing more from his pocket. "Fine. But only one now, and we'll do the rest later."

Skye watched him shake out a wrap onto the kitchenette's worktop. The white powder scattered like spilled sugar over the black granite surface. Andrew cut it into two lines, rolling up a bank note to snort it. At least he didn't ask her to supply the money.

"My turn." She enjoyed the tickling sensation as she inhaled, anticipating the high to follow. Like a sugar rush, the buzz hit her. She danced to the fridge, opening it to remove two cans of vodka and tonic. "Want some?"

"I said no alcohol."

"Going to stop me?" She poured one into a glass, replacing the other in the fridge. "Suit yourself."

"Christ. I'm doing another line."

Andrew didn't share this time. When he'd finished, eyes shining, he produced a pair of handcuffs from his pocket. "Let's go to bed. We'll do your meeting prep afterwards."

"Do you really have to be in charge?" she asked, her tone disingenuous. It was a harmless kink and she had no problem with it, but he should have asked. She was sick of being treated like a servant. Sam wouldn't do that. Even Douglas agreed boundaries.

Andrew laughed. "Doesn't it turn you on? Use them on me if you want." He dangled the restraints in front of her.

Skye snatched them. "I just might." It would take her mind off the impending meeting. Whatever happened there, it would change her life. While success meant untold riches, one false move would send her on a fast track to prison. Andrew regarded jail as an occupational hazard, but she feared it would be an extended nightmare. As in her childhood, she would wake each day to boredom, violence, and a total lack of hope.

Too much was riding on tomorrow. Suddenly light-headed, she knocked back her drink and handed the cuffs back to him.

# CHAPTER 16

## SKYE

In a departure from her usual routine, Skye had spent half the morning making herself look older. A thick pancake foundation covered her peachy skin; bronzer accentuated the hollows of her cheeks. She'd drawn a dark red line around her lips and filled them in with a lighter shade. Her eyes were heavily lined, topped with gelled brows. Finally, she'd donned a dowdy black skirt suit and spectacles with plain lenses.

A breeze whipped through her long dark hair as she walked past St Philip's Cathedral and the elegant stone terraces of Colmore Row. Nearby, a cluster of glass towers reflected the clouds above Birmingham's city centre. The law firm was based in one of these. They occupied one of the higher floors; reassuringly expensive, according to Douglas. He'd told her that he charged his clients top dollar and he had to look the part.

Skye entered a ground floor lobby boasting a marble floor and real trees rooted in marble tubs. She fingered her locks as she entered the revolving door, smoothing the wind's ravages. No one would recognise her, she told herself. On her regular visits to Douglas's office, she'd been blonde, her natural colour. Douglas had introduced her as his niece. She didn't dare ask him if he had other nieces and whether they were over sixteen. In the early days as his sugar baby, she hadn't been.

If he'd met her for the first time today, Douglas wouldn't have given her a second glance. Her appearance blended in with her surroundings. This hive of big business wasn't the kind of place where she felt at ease, however. Like Andrew, Douglas had cautioned her not to betray her humble origins when she paid a call. She'd made sure to speak as little as possible. Now she was grateful that Andrew had told her what to say. He was, of course, familiar with the ways of lawyers, having been in and out of prison all his life.

Stiletto heels drumming on the immaculate floor, she strode to the pale wood reception desk. Her confidence rose at the sight of the young man sitting there in front of a monitor. He was a stranger to her. She could do this.

"Hello," Skye ventured, trying to copy Jenna's snobby accent. It hardly mattered with him, but Andrew had been right to make her practise. Later, her success might rest on removing all trace of Birmingham from her voice.

"Good morning." His smile didn't reach his eyes. He was probably bored, Skye decided. She would be too, waiting all day on lawyers and other spoilt rich people.

"I'm here to meet Lesley Lloyd of Millican Syme," she said.

"What's your name, please?"

She told him and he thanked her. There was the staccato sound of typing on a keyboard in front of the monitor, then he handed her a white plastic oblong, the size and shape of a credit card. "Tap the gate to get through. Take the lift to the ninth floor, through the double doors, and you'll see their reception. They're expecting you."

A middle-aged woman stood by the lifts already, clearly someone who worked there. She was smartly dressed, glancing at her watch and tutting.

A brushed metal door opened with a shudder. The woman walked in first and asked, "Which floor?"

"Nine."

The door clanked shut and the lift whooshed upwards. Skye coughed, hand over mouth to hide her distaste. A strong smell of perfume, floral and old-fashioned, infused the tiny space. The scent dissipated when the woman left on the fourth floor.

Finally, a disembodied female voice announced, "Level Nine". Skye exited, stepping onto a plush grey carpet. The Millican Syme reception desk was the same colour, made of polished steel, with three women sitting behind it. Despite matching red jackets, they appeared barely out of their teens. Perhaps Douglas had chosen them.

Two were deep in conversation with each other. The third bid her a cheery good morning.

"I'm here to see Lesley Lloyd." Her voice was strained, but thankfully, the Birmingham accent didn't emerge.

"Your name?"

"Jenna Wyatt."

That produced a smile. "Yes, she's expecting you. I'll take you to the meeting room."

Skye followed her along a corridor, its cream walls displaying a collection of modern art. The paintings seemed to be random splodges of colour, but Douglas had informed her they were worth millions. His firm didn't own them; they rented pictures for a nominal fee. Millican Syme took a commission if a wealthy client bought a piece.

Skye shook her head. Jenna was missing a trick. In Clifton, the locals had buckets of cash. You could tell by the Porsches parked near the bridge and the Waitrose delivery vans blocking the streets. Perhaps little Miss Perfect didn't want to spoil the appearance of her spotty bunting with someone else's art. More likely, Jenna hadn't even thought of the idea. It was obvious she'd never had to hustle.

"Here we are." Her guide pushed at a door. It glided open noiselessly.

No-one sat inside the square room, which was dominated by a floor to ceiling window. Skye gazed at the view over the city's Jewellery Quarter rooftops, the BT Tower sticking up a finger above them.

"Do sit down, Jenna. Coffee?"

"Yes, please."

"How do you take it?"

What was she meant to say: up her bottom? "Black," she mumbled.

Refreshments were laid out on a cabinet: two sleek chrome pots, white china cups and saucers, a jug of water, glasses, and biscuits in individual wrappers. The young woman poured coffee and suggested Skye help herself to a snack.

Left alone, Skye positioned her back against the door to keep it closed. She took a swig from the vodka bottle in her backpack. It calmed her jitters. Once she'd put it away, she lounged on one of the ugly but comfortable S-shaped chairs which surrounded a central meeting table. Nibbling a finger of shortbread, she gazed out of the window.

In the far distance, she thought she spotted a council tower block where she used to live. It was hard to tell. They all looked the same. She had no affection for it and little for the mother who had dragged her from one home to another. Jenna didn't know she was born.

Skye fidgeted, nerves rising at the notion of impersonating Jenna to Lesley Lloyd, who would be less of a pushover than the receptionists. She filled a water glass with vodka, before reclaiming her seat and allowing the swirly wallpaper to mesmerise her. Shades of blue and grey collided and spun like a choppy sea. The décor was worse than Jenna's café. Had Skye still been pregnant and prone to nausea, it would have tipped her over the edge.

After a ten-minute wait, the lawyer arrived.

"Jenna, so lovely to meet you. I'm Lesley." She extended a hand.

Skye assumed she was supposed to shake it. She stood up, taking Lesley's hand in a weak grip and noting the understated French manicure. Lesley Lloyd defied her expectations. Skye had imagined a young, sharp-suited glamour puss, but Lesley was closer to Douglas in age. She wore a plain grey trouser suit, salt and pepper hair tied back in a bun, and minimal make-up.

"I see you have a drink," Lesley said. "Do sit down and I'll get my own."

She perched across the meeting table from Skye, placing an iPad and a cup of milky coffee in front of her. "I presume you were surprised to find Mitchell Vincent had left you a substantial bequest," she said.

"Yes." Skye tried to copy Jenna's voice again.

"Has anyone mentioned his name to you before?" Lesley's eyes were kind.

Skye recalled the neat piles of documents on Douglas's desk. She knew a lot about the Vincent family, but Jenna didn't. Jenna gushed about Vincent's coffee, but she'd never spoken about Mitchell. "No," she mumbled.

"I understand," Lesley said, "that Mitch Vincent believed himself to be your father." She waited for a reaction.

Skye gawped at her, dismayed to find Lesley so chatty. She hadn't counted on that.

"I'm sorry," Lesley said. "It's clearly a shock."

"Yes." Skye wished Lesley would stop talking and give her the money. She drained the glass of vodka.

"I don't know all the details," Lesley said. "Our senior partner, Douglas Millican, was a close friend of Mitch's and he could have told you more, but he's out of the office today. He asked me to give you his apologies." She spoke of Douglas with devotion. Skye had noticed everyone at Millican Syme treated him like a god; after all, he was the boss here.

Skye swallowed. "No problem." She managed a neutral accent.

"From what I heard, Mitch was a lovely man. Over the years, Millican Syme did a large amount of business with him. Not just estate planning, but commercial deals."

Skye knew this from her trysts in Douglas's office, although she hardly cared. Reluctant to say more than she needed, she nodded.

"Mitch would have liked to know you better, I think, but Sheila was against it."

Skye recognised the name of Mitch's widow. She suspected Sheila was Andrew's latest mark.

"You won't hear from Sheila, but the rest of the family may wish to get in touch," Lesley said. "Would you mind if I share contact details?"

Panicking about her less than perfect diction, Skye pretended to cough. "Sorry, I'd rather not," she spluttered.

"I understand. Mitch took steps to provide for you, of course. May I ask, were you happy with your education?" Lesley's beady brown eyes searched Skye's face.

Jenna had a degree, a business, and an expensive flat, so the answer wasn't difficult. "Yes," Skye said, staring at her untouched coffee. She regretted finishing the vodka. As the beginnings of a tension headache needled her temples, she resented Lesley for drawing her into a conversation. Channelling Jenna as much as she could, she said, "You wrote me a letter?"

"That's right." As if snapping to attention, Lesley sat upright, smile vanishing. "Did they verify your identity earlier?"

"No."

Lesley frowned. "Can I see your documents?"

Skye produced Jenna's passport.

The lawyer examined the photo page. "It's a terrible likeness."

Skye's headache intensified. She stared at Lesley.

"Mine's the same," Lesley said cheerfully. "Unflattering can't begin to describe it, and so grainy that it could be anybody. Do you have proof of address?"

Andrew had either found or faked a water bill. Skye handed it over. She ran her fingers through her glossy dark locks, carefully removing strands she'd pulled from Jenna's hairbrush and plaited into the wig.

"Here," she offered them, "in case you want to run a DNA test."

Lesley's mouth fell open. She laughed. "No, that won't be necessary. I've seen enough."

"You'll need bank details too." Skye passed over a neatly typed sheet. Remembering Andrew's instructions, she added, "Can you arrange a transfer today, please?"

"I'll do my best, but I'll have to find a partner to approve it," Lesley said. "Leave it with me."

Skye couldn't stop a grin creeping over her lips. She'd done it.

86

# CHAPTER 17

# A MAN WITH A PROBLEM

"This is a handsome piece, isn't it?" Sheila said. "I can picture it in the pink room."

He dragged his eyes away from a pretty girl, one of several punters browsing on the day before the auction. With the kind of money Sheila intended to spend, it was advisable to inspect the lots rather than rely on photographs. Harsh fluorescent lights revealed every scratch and woodworm hole. They threw Sheila's wrinkles into sharp relief as well.

"Very interesting," he extemporised. Glancing at the description, he added, "But it's a Queen Anne settle, so I feel it would sit out of place."

She twisted her mouth. "What should I buy then?"

He swept an arm around. "Nothing. Alas, I fear these are all counterfeit."

He almost wished he hadn't lied about his expertise. Despite his extensive knowledge of many subjects, he hadn't paid much attention to Tudor furniture. What he'd seen here was awful: carved from oak, dark and ungainly. The ridiculous guide prices made him laugh.

Just because she lived in a manor of the period, there was no reason to fill it with ugly relics. Nonetheless, it was impossible to deflect her from a fixed idea. He would turn it to his advantage instead. As she was so keen to waste her money, he'd source a few reproduction pieces and make a nice commission. Sheila would never find out.

She hadn't noticed the absence of rare books from her library, either. He'd refilled the shelves with old leather-bound tomes of no value whatsoever. You could buy them by the yard.

A white-haired fellow, dressed eccentrically in a tweed suit and half-moon spectacles, caught his eye. A cold sweat gripped him; he recognised the man as an antiquarian bookseller who had bought several of Mitch's first editions.

There was no avoiding the old codger, so he strode over to him and clapped him on the shoulder. "Septimus! What little treasures have you turned up here?"

Septimus, stooping over a Regency walnut cabinet, replied with some stiffness, "This and that." His gaze settled on Sheila's legs, on display under a short cream leather mini skirt. "Are you going to introduce me to your friend?"

"Sheila – Septimus," he said, annoyed at forgetting not every man was deterred by Sheila's years. She kept herself toned and tanned, after all. Besides, Septimus probably had one foot in the grave. He must be over eighty, an old school dealer who would continue in the trade until they took him out of his shop in a box.

"Enchanted," Septimus murmured.

In a stroke of luck, the old boy then took Sheila's hand and kissed it, which did not impress her at all. She drew away from him as if she'd been stung. Septimus clearly wasn't her type. "I'm so sorry, but we're about to leave," she said.

"Anything tempting you?" Septimus asked, watery eyes twinkling behind his glasses.

"Not in the least." Sheila dropped all pretence of politeness. "It's all fakes."

She stalked off. He shrugged at Septimus, whispering, "Women, eh?" before following her.

It was more entertaining than a trip to Edinburgh. He permitted himself a chuckle. As he left the auction house and made small talk with Sheila, he imagined his rival sitting red-eyed on an early train. Perhaps he'd travelled yesterday, breakfasted in a dull hotel, and was waiting for the meeting that wouldn't happen. It was ironic how their paths had crossed as they'd wooed the merry widow. In a rare moment of introspection, he saw the other man as his nemesis.

McPherson, still receiving weekly instalments, was a more likely candidate. Even so, today he would finally be free of the noose tying him to McPherson and the other creditors. His plans were coming to fruition. Once the cash hit Skye's bank account, the only remaining hurdle would be removing it.

His little sugar baby, professionally compliant, usually did as she was told. He sensed this would be different, though. She'd need persuading.

After leaving Sheila, he bought a magnum of champagne. Then he visited a man who owed him a favour. The encounter with Skye wasn't going to end well for her, but he hoped she'd make it easy on herself. He'd always had a soft spot for Skye.

# CHAPTER 18

## SKYE

She'd paid until the end of the week, but if the money arrived today, she'd leave the Airbnb tomorrow morning. Twitchily, Skye slouched on the sofa, swiping her phone to check the banking app. The account was in her new name, Jenna Wyatt, as it had been ever since Skye changed it by deed poll.

That had been Andrew's idea. It meant they could use Skye's existing bank account, which she'd had for years. Andrew said it was important in convincing the lawyers that she really was Jenna. So was the passport. He'd talked a good game, and the meeting at Millican Syme had appeared to go well, but had the plan really worked? There was only one way to find out.

Skye's jaw dropped. She counted the digits. Her bank balance stood at over two million pounds. Giggling, she kissed the screen.

This called for a celebration. Skye picked up a silvery knife from the block sitting on the kitchenette's granite worktop. She cut a lemon into six slices, placing two of them in a glass. To this, she added an ice cube and a can of vodka and tonic.

"Cheers." Skye raised the glass to herself, knocking back its contents. She followed it with a line of Andrew's coke, carefully arranged on the black granite. A bottle of vodka and a nos canister were fine if she had nothing else, but she preferred to go upmarket.

Now she must wait for Andrew, travelling back from Edinburgh after his meeting with Douglas. Bored, she made another drink, took more coke, and paced around the room. She opened the French doors, then thought better of it as a breeze tickled her shoulders. Earlier, she'd sat outside to vape, but the chilly weather had deterred her from staying long. Her wig, spectacles, and suit had been discarded in favour of a strappy top and tight jeans.

Skye turned up the heating, glanced at the view, and looked away. The scenery was unimpressive compared with her bedroom at Jenna's place. At night, she had enjoyed gazing at the suspension bridge, its filaments lit up like skeins of jewels. That, and Sam's presence, were her brightest memories of Bristol. Andrew had been good in bed too, she supposed.

Maybe she'd continue to see him once the job was done, but she probably wouldn't bother. After they split the cash, she would do as she pleased. Sleeping with men her own age was top of her bucket list. She could return to Bristol and snatch Sam from his dull girlfriend. It would be weird bumping into Jenna again, but maybe she didn't need to. If she lurked outside the cupcakery, Sam would eventually emerge to vape. Anyway, Jenna didn't know about the money and would never find out.

She and Andrew had agreed on equal shares. Should she trust him? His criminal record suggested not, but what choice did she have? Perhaps she should make tracks now, before he returned. Two million pounds was better than one. If she skipped town, how would he ever find her?

The answer hit her like an unpleasant smell. Whatever Douglas said, Skye didn't plan on going to ground in Panama. She would be living it up. Suppose she and Sam were photographed on the red carpet together? Andrew would see the image and hunt her down. He wouldn't even need to do it himself; he'd been inside so many times, for so many frauds, that he'd built a solid criminal network. What would happen to her, with a price on her head? Skye shuddered, realising she couldn't expect mercy. It wasn't worth the risk. Far better to hand over his share, then put their partnership behind her.

A bell rang. With a jolt, Skye realised it was the door.

"Yeah?" she spoke to the intercom.

"Hello, Skye."

Puzzled, she said, "I thought you'd gone to Edinburgh."

"Well, I didn't. Are you letting me in?"

She buzzed him inside the block and waited by the door as his footsteps clattered up the staircase.

He brandished a magnum of champagne in one hand. "You clever girl," he said, kissing her on the lips.

She gaped at him. He was no mirage, but, "How—"

"I didn't need to go. It was enough for your friend to think I would. Imagine him sitting in that hotel lobby, in his best suit, waiting. I bet he's still there now." He laughed.

Skye managed an answering titter.

"You started partying already," he said, his eyes alighting on the shiny knife.

A flicker of unease tensed her shoulders as his gaze lingered on the blade. Apart from domination in the bedroom, he'd never displayed signs of violence, but there was always a first time. Perhaps she should strike now, neutralise the threat. The block of knives gleamed in the room's spotlights. She weighed up her chances of sticking one in his ribs.

90

Years ago, she'd seen it done. A pair of boys at her school, fourteen-year-olds, had been fighting. With the battle signalled in advance, a hungry audience gathered, whooping as the larger lad pinned his enemy to the ground. Then the cheers grew louder. The underdog had pulled out a switchblade.

There was so much blood. Skye hadn't yelled encouragement anymore. She'd stumbled away, retching. The memory still brought bile to her throat. She couldn't kill a man, especially someone for whom she felt a degree of warmth. It would be kidding both of them to call it love.

How would she even dispose of a corpse? More likely, lacking expertise in stabbing, she'd fail in her attempt. He'd survive and he'd be angry.

She was panicking for nothing, she told herself. "I'll find wine glasses," she offered.

"Well, I'll make myself comfortable. Why don't we sit out on the balcony and have a drink looking out over the water?"

Marching to the French doors, he threw them open. The sounds of the canal, a barge chugging, and seagulls screeching, filtered into the room along with a damp breeze. Skye shivered.

"Perhaps we'll stay in, nice and cosy." He closed the outsize windows again. "Birmingham has more canals than Venice. Did you know that? I bet you learned at school."

Skye nodded. She'd heard the factoid before, although she didn't remember where. Even when she'd bothered to attend, her odyssey through the city's schools hadn't taught her a great deal.

She held out two tulip-shaped flutes. "Are you opening that fizz?"

"Of course." He walked to the sink, found a towel, and expertly removed the cork with a muffled boom. "Bottoms up!"

Skye savoured the prickle of bubbles on her tongue. It was excellent champagne, although she'd expect nothing less from him.

He topped up her glass, his attention returning to the view. "You wouldn't believe how this area has changed. When I was a boy, you'd see shopping trolleys dumped in the waterways. Dead dogs, even."

Silence hung in the air as he stared at the canal.

# CHAPTER 19

## JENNA

Roads in Bristol's Temple Quay business zone had ancient names like Anvil Street and Old Bread Street. The buildings were tall and recent. Since I left, the insurance company had moved from a chilly 1960s office block to a new build five minutes from the station. Beth liked it because she could take the train to work.

The location impressed me less. On this blustery day, the new skyscrapers created a wind tunnel. A swell of air tried to sweep me off my feet. It didn't help that I rarely wore heels anymore and tottered awkwardly.

For this interview, I'd adopted the bland corporate look that I hated. My makeup was discreet, my trouser suit a boring navy, and my wild hair tamed by a French pleat. I needed a job. The extra capital I'd borrowed was disappearing at an alarming rate, mostly to service my debt. The rent I'd expected to collect from Andrew for a few months was no more than a mirage. Part of what he'd paid had even been disputed by the credit card companies. There was no point selling my car: I'd tried a couple of websites who claimed to buy anything, but it would raise little more than a hundred pounds. No options remained except a return to insurance.

The company had reorganised. Our last boss had left, and Beth was now working for Hal, a high flyer who had joined on the same graduate programme as us. I'd always found his intensity irritating, but Beth spoke highly of him as a manager. He obviously remembered me, because he'd fixed an interview straight away when she said I longed to come back.

Although the premises were different, I had a sense of déjà vu when I entered through the revolving door. Sally, the matronly receptionist, greeted me with a smile.

"Jenna, it's been a long time. Had enough of cupcakes?"

"You should see my waistline." I patted it. The white lie spared me humiliation. I needn't admit to her that my big business idea hadn't been so clever after all. As soon I had a job offer in the bag, I'd hand in the café's keys to my landlord.

Sally twisted her face ruefully. "Know the feeling," she said, "although look at you. A breeze would blow you away." She handed me a visitor's card on a lanyard and advised that Hal's PA would escort me to his office.

A giant black and white photo of the suspension bridge covered the wall behind her, no doubt to impress visitors. Sally herself had a view of the lobby and, through the window, a hotel across the road. While she dealt with more callers, I sat on a leather couch with square ends, flicking through social media on my phone. The reception copy of the 'Financial Times' remained untouched. I was surprised the firm still bought it.

Ten minutes after the appointed time, the PA arrived. "Hal says sorry he's late, but he had to take a phone call." She sounded out of breath. "I'm Angelika, by the way, and I joined last week. Hal says you worked here before?"

Petite and fresh out of university, she was enthusiastic about the company. We chatted in the lift, Angelika using it as an opportunity to take my coffee order. There was a barista in the top floor canteen, apparently, and he made the best beverages in Bristol. I didn't have the heart to explain that I offered strong competition.

Situated on a corner of the building, Hal's office resembled a giant ice cube. It was surrounded by glass on four sides: two external windows and two internal ones looking out over an open plan area. Beth sat in one of the cramped rows of desks. She waved to me.

Hal, whose ginger buzz cut had been barely visible behind a monitor, stood up. Observing him tower over Angelika, I recalled how tall he always seemed.

His gaze flicked in Beth's direction, eyes softening, but he made no comment about her. "Great to see you again, Jenna," he said, extending a hand. "Angelika, my usual, please."

She left and Hal gestured to a circular meeting table with four chairs around it. When I'd chosen one, he manoeuvred his lanky frame into the seat opposite.

"So," he said, steepling his fingers under his firm jaw, "you'd like your old job back?"

"Yes." A chill crept across my shoulders as I lied. "I really miss insurance."

"Naturally you would," Hal said, without irony. "There's been a lot of change in the last three years, though. We've had a transformation programme. Much of the corporate client work has been automated, doubling the number of cases that executives are expected to handle. Space has been streamlined too. Everyone is hot desking—"

"Except you," I interrupted.

"C-suite and above have their own offices." He smirked.

I was reminded why I didn't like him. "Anyway?" I prompted.

"Anyway, you'll recall I moved to HQ in London after six months with the company. I was tasked with delivering efficiency savings, which I did, exceeding my targets by fifty per cent. As a result, I was headhunted to lead a team here and grow both top and bottom line. The first quarter is looking promising."

"Good," I said, non-plussed. It sounded like he was dictating his CV rather than showing an interest in mine.

"I'll get to the point. You'll have seen the article about this company in today's 'Financial Times'?"

Inwardly, I rebuked myself for not glancing at the paper when I had the chance. I couldn't blag my way out of this. "Not yet," I admitted.

Hal coughed. "I see. Well, the share price rose thirty per cent yesterday. There are rumours of a bid. We'll need to optimise profitability. I understand the Board met earlier and decided to implement a hiring freeze."

I flinched. "What are you telling me?"

Hal's expression seemed genuinely regretful. "I'd like to bring you into my team, but it's impossible at this moment in time." He added, "Sorry."

I gasped, more in relief than dismay. "I don't understand why you asked me to come in. I mean, if there isn't a position here—"

Hal cut across me. "I thought there was, until thirty minutes ago. Just before you arrived, I had a phone call from HR. Be assured, I did my best to change their minds, but it's not happening. This is an edict from the top, I'm afraid."

Angelika returned with two coffees in cardboard cups. Having no desire to stay and exchange small talk with Hal, I stood up and reached out to take one. "Thanks. I'll drink it on the way out."

"This is yours. Straight up latte. Hal, here's your skinny vanilla soy macchiato."

"Perfect," Hal said. "Angelika, we've finished our meeting. Can you show Jenna out?"

"Sure." An eyebrow twitched in surprise, then she collected herself and smiled brightly.

Hal shook my hand again. Uncannily, I detected sympathy in his touch. Perhaps he was basically a decent sort.

"Should the situation change, I'll be in contact," he promised. "You know, we spent a very brief period working together, but I enjoyed it. I'll do what I can. If anyone leaves, I could maybe make a case."

"Thanks." The prospect of a return appealed even less than it had an hour ago. There was every chance I would end up tied to a desk once more, but would it come in time to pay the mortgage?

Angelika ushered me out of the glass cube. Beth winked at me, evidently thinking the job offer was a done deal. I shook my head, hoping Angelika wouldn't notice. As I said goodbye to her and left the building, I turned my head away from the picture of the bridge. It seemed like a sick joke, taunting me with everything I was about to lose.

Out of the wind and cocooned in my car again, I warmed my trembling hands on the cup and sipped the coffee. It was strong and subtly flavoured. While I didn't blame Angelika for raving about it, nothing beat the smoothness of Vincent's roast beans. My lattes were better.

# CHAPTER 20

## SKYE

Skye stretched lazily in the comfortable bed. The magnum was empty. She'd had most of it, and another line of coke, then spent a wild hour between crisp white cotton sheets. It was the sweetest, most tender experience she'd ever had with him. For once, it seemed he'd been focused on her pleasure rather than requiring her to please him. Woozily, she snuggled against his naked body.

"Skye?"

His voice seemed far away, but affectionate. That pleased her. She savoured the moment. "Mmm," she mumbled.

"We should go away together."

Skye found it hard to concentrate on the idea. Unease nagged her, a warning to ignore him, but her dulled senses couldn't pinpoint the problem. How much had she drunk? She hadn't been counting.

All she really wanted to do was sleep. "Not now," she muttered.

He snapped on his bedside lamp.

The intense white light hurt her eyes. She shielded them with her hands, regarding him through her fingers. "Turn it off," she moaned.

Ignoring her, he stood up, stretching and yawning. He pulled on his underwear, shirt, and trousers. "Look, I'll help you pack," he said.

"Later. Sleeping now."

He flicked a switch, bringing the ceiling bulb into life.

"Too bright," Skye complained.

"Is that your only luggage?" He pointed to a small animal print Samsonite, her weekend bag.

"Yes… don't have much."

"Whatever." Impatiently, he grabbed her clothes from the wardrobe and began stuffing them into the Samsonite. "Get dressed. Then we can make sure the money's safe."

Since he'd strolled into the Airbnb, this was the first time he'd mentioned the cash. Her mouth fell open. "But, 's fine. In the bank." Through a fog of drowsiness, she wondered why he was so edgy.

"It's too easily traced in the UK. We need to transfer it to a foreign bank account. Then we'll treat ourselves to a trip abroad and spend it. You've got that passport, haven't you?"

She couldn't process the information. How did a passport matter? "It, it, it's not mine. Jenna's," she gabbled.

"You persuaded an eagle-eyed lawyer it was yours. A border guard would never notice. Come on, time is of the essence."

Skye's stomach fluttered. She must have overdone the champagne. It had slipped down so easily, she'd guzzled it like fizzy pop. "Feel sick," she said.

"You'll be fine." He lifted her shoulders to a sitting position. Propping her against the bedhead, he picked up her discarded garments from the floor and eased them onto her. He struggled to zip up the skinny jeans, panting with the effort. His face lit up when he succeeded. "That wasn't so bad, was it?" he said. "Come into the lounge. I'll make coffee."

She supposed she needed it. To her surprise, once she'd dangled her feet over the edge of the bed, she found she could stand. Unsteadily, she padded after him, curling up on the sofa.

He made her black instant coffee. Setting it on the coffee table, he passed Skye's phone to her.

"Open your banking app."

Suddenly, her fingers wouldn't work. She fumbled, dropping the phone.

"You did that on purpose," he accused.

Why was his tone so shrill? Still, he looked adorable when angry, hair sticking up at odd angles and gaze fixed on hers. She giggled.

"Why's it important?" she protested. "Sleepy. Go back bed."

Huffing, he retrieved her phone from the floor. "You're lucky you didn't break it. Try again."

She succeeded on the second attempt.

"Now, give it back to me."

Skye tittered. "All right. Can I sleep now?"

"Soon." He whistled, eyes widening as he observed the screen. "Oh yes. You clever thing."

No comment seemed to be required. Skye reached for her coffee mug, knocking it to the floor. The white porcelain shattered, brown liquid puddling at her feet. "Oops," she said.

She ought to clean it, but her limbs refused to shift more than an inch. They appeared glued to the sofa. It was weird.

He hardly glanced at the mess, which disconcerted her, as he was usually fastidious. "I'll get a towel in a minute," he said. "Where's your card reader?"

She gestured to the bedroom, her movements slow.

"And what's your PIN?"

"One. Two. Three. Four," she enunciated, adding, "Nosy."

"What?" He squinted at her, as if the sounds were incoherent. "Say again?"

She tried.

"I think I've got it. One two three four. Amazing." He disappeared into the other room, emerging a few minutes later with a broad smile. "All done. Who's my good girl?"

"Sleepy girl," Skye said.

"Quite. I need to sober up, and I think you do too. Let's go for a walk in the moonlight."

He helped her stand and shuffle out of the apartment, into the lift, and outside. She shivered in the November chill.

He put his arms around her. "Is that better?"

"Yes." The cold air awakened her slowly. She was still groggy, leaning into him. His embrace was enjoyable, though, and the setting romantic. A full moon reflected in the canal, splitting into a thousand shimmering fragments.

"Diamonds," she said.

"What?" he said, and laughed. "Like some, huh? I bet you would."

They walked along the towpath and across an arched bridge, she stumbling and he propping her up. There were bars nearby and she heard echoes of revelry. It reassured Skye that she wasn't alone.

"This is just like Venice. You've never been, have you? Should I return, I'll remember this moment with you," he said.

"I could come too." She had Jenna's passport. He'd said something about using it, hadn't he, so why not go somewhere pretty? Notions of gondoliers and ice cream flitted into her fuddled brain. She clutched his hand.

They staggered past locks, the path gradually sloping down into a tunnel below a road. The mossy walls and dank smell closed in on Skye. She was relieved when they emerged into fresh air. Here, the buildings on either side of the canal were tall, covered in plastic shrouds which flapped in the breeze. Strangely, her addled brain recalled a TV news item; these were new builds which had to be stripped of cladding, shiny and deadly.

She shivered in reaction to the reminder of death and the sharp, freezing air. This wasn't fun anymore. "Can we go back?" she asked.

"Soon."

Entering another tunnel, she barely made out the shape of a lock gate ahead. The silence was tangible, like a beast trying to choke her. There was no longer evidence of upmarket flats and bars; they were part of a different city, in another world.

A stench of rot and urine tickled her nostrils. Skye coughed. Her foot stubbed at something soft. If her companion hadn't been supporting her, she would have tripped.

"Spare change?" the bundle at her feet whined hopefully.

Skye recoiled, while secretly grateful to see another person. "I don't have any," she said.

"Who uses cash these days?"

The scorn was obvious, and not just to Skye. As she shrank back, the beggar lurched unsteadily to his feet, wagging a grimy finger at the couple.

"You think you're better than me, is that it?" Sour alcoholic fumes emerged as he spat out the words.

To Skye's horror, the stranger's teeth were mere stumps, but that wasn't what disturbed her most. Although scruffy, the vagrant was young, his skin unlined and spotty with acne.

Shrinking from him, she patted her sides. The youth couldn't steal from her; she hadn't brought any belongings. Through her brain fog, she recollected needing keys for the flat.

At that moment, the lad threw a punch.

It wasn't aimed at Skye, but she ducked anyway, slipping, and falling onto the cold, damp path. "Help," she whimpered, noting with shock that she was unable to make a louder sound.

"Hush, Skye. I'll protect you."

Scrambling to her feet, she saw her companion had evaded the blow too. Coolly, he reached into his pocket. Perhaps he had money after all. Would the beggar leave them alone then? She cringed, assessing her chances of running back to the city above, to the shiny nightspots where no-one cared about dangers lurking under the surface.

She tried a single uncertain step, wobbled, and steadied herself against the tunnel wall. Her companion grinned. Instead of bringing out money, he thrust his empty hand into their attacker's chest, and pushed.

It was over so quickly. The young man toppled backwards, the dark canal claiming him with a splash.

99

Skye stared, dazed, as he flailed. His fingers scrabbled in vain to gain purchase on the forbidding walls rising from the water's edge. A scream turned into a horrible gurgling sound as he sank into the depths.

"Why?" she asked, her words emerging as a whisper. Maybe it hadn't really happened. She would wake up in the morning, alone in the cosy flat.

"The end justifies the means," he said. "Don't you agree?"

Skye was about to protest, but he brought his face towards hers, as if to kiss her. No sweetness touched her lips, however. She felt, rather than saw, the pressure of his fist against her stomach. The brief, intense moment of pain passed. She fell, tumbling downwards.

Skye yelped. Her gelled fingernails scraped against bricks. No sooner had her feet felt the first shock of ice-cold water, than it was all around her, seeping into her nose and mouth and ears.

She gasped. Her chest burned. She couldn't breathe, or even move to struggle for air. Then she couldn't sense anything at all.

# CHAPTER 21

## JENNA

Perhaps it was my shaky finances, or maybe his disappearance had knocked my confidence, but I found myself reaching for booze more often after Andrew left. My first act on arriving home each evening was to treat myself to a glass of cheap dry white. One drink led to another. This morning, a headache pulsed through my temples as I unlocked the café.

Pumpkin spice cupcakes featured on the menu today. I'd bought the flavoured syrup for coffee when Halloween was on the horizon. It hadn't sold well, so I'd decided to try it in my baking. The café was warm and sweetly scented by the time Sam arrived at half past eight.

He rubbed his eyes, as if he'd caught my hangover, but then smiled. "Smells good."

I took the hint. "Pumpkin spice with cream cheese and candied orange. Want to try?"

"Need you ask?"

I chose the least perfect cake, its swirl of icing slightly off centre, and placed it on a plate for him.

"Lush. Just what I needed."

"Everything okay?"

Sam sighed. "I still haven't heard on my last audition. My agent says it's down to me and one other guy."

"You really wanted this one, didn't you?"

"Who wouldn't? Three months in the south of France, all expenses paid."

"Beth will miss you."

He pursed his lips. "I can't limit myself to jobs in Bristol. She knows that."

A surge of customers suddenly arrived: mothers who had dropped off children at school, office workers getting takeouts and even the gym bunny. I had learned she was called Kimberley. Sam greeted all of them, valiantly upselling where possible, but his liveliness seemed feigned.

My phone rang. Hoping it was Andrew calling to confirm he'd settle his unpaid rent, I checked the screen and saw a number I didn't recognise. Before I swiped to answer, Sam passed me a large order. The day flew by. I'd almost forgotten the call when, finally, I had a chance to make myself a coffee and check messages.

"It's Grace Vincent," the voicemail began. "Jenna, I know you're not keen to meet, but I'd really like to, and we're having a gathering to celebrate Dad's life. It's this Monday and it would be amazing if you could make it. Two o'clock at Bruntney Manor. Bring a friend if you like." Her tones were posh and breathless. "Ring me back and say you'll come. Please."

If it was really the designer herself, she'd surely rung the wrong person. "Sam," I called him over, set the message to replay and handed him the phone, "Listen to this."

His eyes widened. "I don't get it."

"Me neither. It's a scam, isn't t? That surely isn't Grace. You know her, so what do you think?"

Sam sucked his teeth. "Her voice is distinctive and it certainly sounded like her. Not that I'd bet money on it, though. It's easy enough to copy someone. I mean, even Skye can do that."

I flushed. When Skye impersonated me, she'd produced a caricature. "I just don't understand why Grace Vincent, dressmaker to the stars, would invite me to a bash. And where's this manor house, anyway? She just assumed I'd know what she was talking about."

Sam laughed. "Grace is so ditsy."

"And how would she know my number?"

"It's on your website, and Vincent's Coffee have it, don't they?" Sam touched my arm. "I bet they're buttering up all their customers now that Old Man Vincent has died. That's why they've asked you to a jolly."

I digested the information. "I'd forgotten Grace was connected to those Vincents. You say one of them has died?"

"I heard all about it from her. She cried on my shoulder a couple of times," Sam said. "Her dad lost his life halfway up a mountain. He was a Munro bagger—"

Bewildered, I asked, "What's that?"

"A madman who yearns to climb every Scottish mountain over three thousand feet high. I think there are around two hundred and eighty of them, and Mitch Vincent had started on his last fifty. Unfortunately, he had a heart attack and they couldn't get him medical attention in time. Grace was in bits."

I nodded, recalling that fateful visit from the police. "I know how that feels."

"Yes, you had it rough," Sam agreed. "Not only with your mum dying, but then Richard being an arse. He pulled you out of that posh school to make you slave away in his B&B."

"Even worse, he let me do A levels locally, and I met you."

"Every cloud has a silver lining." Sam smirked. "Luckily for Grace, her mum is still around, and she has siblings – brothers, I think. One of them runs the family food business. It's not just coffee, either. Mitch built quite an empire. Grace doesn't have to worry about money, at least."

"So she's a trust fund kid. Nice for her," I commented. "I don't know her from Adam, though, and I still don't see why she would phone me with a message like that. It sounded so personal."

Sam shrugged. "That's just her way. Lovely, but everything's terribly, terribly exciting, you know? I expect she's just helping out. She told me that Mitch made all his kids work for him when they were young. He thought it kept them grounded."

"Did it?"

"I guess. Grace is pretty chilled. Anyway, you should go. It's a chance to network."

I was about to point out that I didn't need to network when Sam asked, "Could I be your plus one? I'd like to see Grace again. She's thick with the producer of the project I just auditioned for. Perhaps I could persuade her to put in a word."

"Can't you just phone her? You said she'd cried on your shoulder."

Sam folded his arms. "She was a tad drunk," he admitted. "We're not best mates, really."

How could I deny him a shot at that breakthrough? "I get it," I said. "You mean you want to network with Grace. No problem. The café's closed on Monday, so I've got no excuse."

Sam gave me the thumbs up. "Thanks, Jenna. Will you call her back now?"

"Nope."

He raised an eyebrow. "Why not?"

"Because you're going to ring her and RSVP for me."

# CHAPTER 22

## JENNA

All my regulars knew Sam was waiting to hear about his breakthrough role. Kimberley asked him about it every day. I suspected that, like a lottery winner, he wouldn't turn up for work at the café if he'd had his dream offer.

He was serving Kimberley her skinny cappuccino when his phone rang. It was set to silent, but the vibration made a grunting noise. Kimberley must have had ears like a fox to hear it over Dua Lipa's warble.

"Hey, Sam, you should answer that. Might be your lucky break," she advised him.

I was in my usual spot behind the counter, manning the espresso machine. As Sam glanced up at me, I nodded, clocking the speed at which he swiped his phone. This call was the real deal.

"Sam Farrow here." He stood up straight, apprehension mingling with hope on his face. Reaching with his free hand, he swept a lock of fair hair back into his man bun.

Sam listened for twenty seconds or so, his half-smile turning into a full-blown, dazzling headlights, wide beam. "That's great news, mate. Thanks. Yes, I'll deal with that email right away."

He waited until he'd ended the call before punching the air. His triumphant cry could have been heard in the next street. "I got the part, people! Hollywood, here I come."

"Surely the south of France?" I said.

Kimberley stood up to hug him. They danced around the café in a gleeful embrace, her grin as broad as Botox would allow. "Well done. Drinks are on you," she said, obviously longing to be invited.

"Yes, I'll be taking my girlfriend out tonight," Sam said, extracting himself. "Jenna, mind if I phone her now?"

"No problem," I said. "I'm really chuffed for you."

Peeking at Kimberley for signs of disappointment, I barely noticed a twitch. It could have been the paralysing effect of botulin, but I suspected she was genuinely elated for him.

Still radiating excitement, Sam went outside. After he'd made a brief phone call, he stared into the distance, vaping.

The illuminated suspension bridge shone against the night sky. Alone on the sofa with my second glass of Pinot Grigio, I chewed over the day's news. I'd need to find a new employee, but maybe one of Sam's actor friends could help. Kimberley and the rest of his fan club might come back then. Skye would have a shock if she returned. Her presence would be both unexpected and unwelcome, even if it meant more rent from her father. Reflecting on the improbability of Andrew breaking radio silence, I finished the glass and reached for the bottle. At least now the pair had left, wine no longer disappeared when my back was turned.

To his credit, Sam had stayed until his shift ended at five. Despite my scepticism, he'd promised to see me in the morning. I hoped he'd have a boozy evening with Beth, perhaps even get down on one knee now he'd made the big time at last. My sense of anticipation rose when my phone rang and I saw it was her.

"Hi, Beth."

I heard weeping.

"Beth, what's wrong?"

"I can't believe it. The bastard," she wailed.

I suddenly felt stone-cold sober. Had Sam had an accident? Not all motorists showed consideration towards cyclists. Sam had come off his bike a couple of times in the past, brushing off his injuries as 'just a scratch'.

"Tell me what happened," I demanded.

"He's dumped me."

"Sam? You're kidding."

She simply sobbed in reply.

"I'll come over," I said. Grabbing another bottle from the kitchen, I called an Uber.

It was a ten-minute journey to Beth's cottage in Montpelier, but it felt much longer. The cab bypassed the city centre, taking a shortcut through the twisting residential streets of Cotham and Redland. These were terraces of huge stone houses, student havens where Sam and I had attended twenty-four-hour house parties. I'd met Ned at one of them. That had been a wild night and I'd even shared a drunken kiss with Sam before Ned had arrived, looking dangerous in a black leather jacket.

105

I never knew why a merchant banker was hanging out with students. Ned had told me he was visiting a cousin. More likely, he'd scented fresh meat: girls younger and more naïve than his usual targets. With me, he got exactly what he wanted. Whether it was a search for a father figure as Sam claimed, or too much alcohol, I'd been drawn to Ned's air of sophistication.

I bit back tears, remembering our fun times together. Ned had convinced me he was the one, spending every other weekend with me and moving in during the pandemic. In the spring of 2020, we'd walked together to Observatory Hill, the old fort where the suspension bridge lay in a panorama below. There, he'd produced a bottle of Cristal, two glasses and a brass padlock. After fixing the latter to the railings at the top of the Avon Gorge, he'd poured out the bubbly. These were symbols of the gold and diamond ring he wanted to buy me as soon as his favourite jewellers reopened. Then he asked me to marry him.

Fool that I was, I said yes.

Now the padlock sat rusting on the hill. Sam had helped me negotiate a fair price for the ring at a pawnbroker. Ned had left me with a painful STD and massive debts. An on-off girlfriend in London had welcomed him back with open arms. She'd always been in the background, but I'd ignored the signs.

I sniffed. Ned was a player, and I was better off without him, but that knowledge didn't stop me missing him. I understood Beth's pain, even if I couldn't fathom Sam's behaviour.

The taxi arrived at Beth's terrace. As on the slopes of Cliftonwood, each house was differently colour-washed. Hers was lilac. It looked stunning in the summer, when lavender bloomed in her front garden. Now the scented flowers had faded and only dry sticks remained.

Clutching the cheap wine like a talisman, I rang the doorbell.

Lewis, one of her lodgers, answered.

"Where's Beth?" I asked sharply.

"In the kitchen," he whispered. "I've been keeping an eye on her. Marc and I are so worried."

"I'm sure she won't do anything daft," I told him. "I'm glad you're here for her."

"And we're glad you've made it over." Relief was written on his face. "The situation needs a woman's touch."

I didn't necessarily agree on that, but Beth could do without the company of a loved-up couple. Lewis and Marc planned to marry and move out. Beth had been delighted for them when they broke the news. Now, their happiness was a mocking contrast to her current mood.

I tiptoed to the kitchen, a pretty, country-style room at the rear of the house. She sat slumped at the pine table, head in her hands.

"Oh, Beth." With my free arm, I hugged her, noting the reddened eyes and whiff of something stronger than wine.

"Thanks for coming round." She clung to me. "Is that pinot?"

"Yes. Warm, I'm afraid. Stick it in the freezer for five minutes."

"It's over there." She pointed. "Lew gave me shots, but I'm still not pissed enough."

"We'll put that right soon," I promised her, pulling up a chair once the wine was cooling. "Want to talk about it?"

"Sam got the part he wanted. We were both thrilled."

"Yes, it's great news."

"I came home early. I had champagne, candles, a ready meal. The full works. Lew and Marc went to the pub, so it would be just the two of us."

I clocked the empty bottle on the worktop.

"I drank it," Beth said. Her face flushed even more. "After I'd proposed and Sam said no."

My jaw dropped. "That was brave of you," I faltered, wishing Sam had matched her courage and accepted.

"He's in love with someone else."

The room seemed to spin. Sam hadn't given me the slightest hint he was cheating on Beth. No wonder she was blotting out her misery with booze.

"Who?" I asked.

"All I know is it's a girl from his work. He wouldn't give me her name, or say how long it's been going on. I must be blind. Literally, I had no idea."

"Don't beat yourself up. I didn't know either. And I didn't twig Ned was unfaithful."

Like Beth, I'd blamed myself for my gullibility. The clues had been there. Apart from the long days of lockdown, Ned had kept his distance. His social media accounts were private. He'd always visited me in Bristol rather than inviting me to London, saying the capital was too high speed for chilling.

Sam's behaviour hadn't appeared suspicious, though. "Sam's always bigging you up. He doesn't talk about anyone else. Unless it's Grace Vincent?"

I nearly stopped myself. Sam had raved about Grace to Kimberley, but he'd also practically begged me to engineer a meeting. They couldn't be close, or he would have just picked up the phone. Then again, if it wasn't an affair but a crush, his actions made sense.

Beth huffed. "I've never heard of Grace Vincent."

"She's friends with his film producer."

Scowling, Beth shook her head. "No, it's someone at your café."

"He flirts with all the ladies, but it's an act." It wasn't quite true, though. I swallowed a sudden surge of bile. Until she vanished, Sam and Skye had laughed and whispered together for hours each day. Could they have crossed a line?

My stomach convulsed at the notion of my childhood friend with a girl who hadn't yet left her childhood behind.

Beth stared at me. "Reckon the wine's cold enough?"

"Absolutely. I'll help you drink it."

# CHAPTER 23

## JENNA

This time I'd gone too far. My phone alarm awoke me to a dry mouth and splitting headache. Groaning, I swiped to snooze.

Ten minutes later, the relentless beeping began again. I dragged myself out of bed, took paracetamol and hoped a cold shower would banish my hangover. Today, I needed to be on top of my game. Although Sam had promised to come to work, I couldn't believe he'd show his face after what he'd done to Beth. I'd be on my own.

After gulping two mugs of instant coffee, I hastened to the café and made batches of the easiest recipes I knew. Chocolate ganache cakes always went down well. Half the customers adored cheese and Marmite muffins while the others hated them, but they were on the lunch menu because I could bake them on autopilot.

To my surprise, Sam parked his bicycle outside at eight thirty.

"Hey," he said, hanging his anorak and helmet behind the counter, "I got my bike back. Life's looking up."

"For you, maybe," I muttered.

"I asked the neighbourhood kids to find it. A tenner, no questions asked. Are you okay? You look tired."

"I got pissed with Beth last night."

He looked sheepish.

"You dumped her. Why?" I glared at him.

"She didn't tell you?" Sam sighed. "When I went home last night, I wanted to party. Beth had a different plan. Discussing our future." He grimaced. "It brought matters to a head. I've been avoiding the truth for a long time—"

"—Because you could live there rent-free," I interjected.

"I'm not proud of leeching off her. That's not why I stayed, though. I'm fond of Beth and didn't want to hurt her."

"So why last night? She's devastated."

"Because she asked for a commitment I can't make."

"You must have known she expected it. Getting engaged is the obvious next step. You've been stringing her along." Heat flushed my face.

"I admit it. I don't love her. I should have left years ago, to let her find a man who would."

109

"Instead, you had an affair."

His voice cracked. "Beth's accusing me of that? It isn't true."

"But you're in love with another girl." Spotting Kimberley, the gym bunny, I pasted a smile on my face and hissed, "We'll talk later."

I fumbled with the coffee machine, scalding myself on the steamer. While Sam could fall back on his acting skills, my edginess showed. It took a major effort to make the right drinks and speak brightly to the customers. The cupcakery's trade had turned the corner, which ordinarily would have been a source of relief. Today, it meant I was rushed off my feet and my headache intensified. I took ibuprofen as well as paracetamol, declining Kimberley's offer of a homeopathic pill. What I really needed was more wine. I glowered at Sam until he began avoiding my gaze.

At five, when we closed, he grabbed his things and walked past me without making eye contact.

"Hey, where are you going?" I asked.

"Bruce's place. I'll be sleeping on the floor, like last night." His shoulders slumped and he turned to look at me. "I didn't mean to end it like that," he said softly. "I like Beth a lot. She deserves better."

"No kidding."

"Can we still be friends?"

I squirmed. "Guess so." It was an evasive answer, because truthfully, I wasn't sure. Beth's woeful tale had thrown Sam's integrity into doubt. Despite his dodgy family, he'd always appeared straightforward and kind. Yet, like Ned, he had a devious side. I wondered if I'd ever really known him.

He seemed satisfied with my reply. "Good," he said.

"I don't suppose you'll want to go to Bruntney Manor now?" I asked. "If Grace is your producer's girlfriend, you'll see plenty of her in France."

"She's not his girlfriend. They're buddies."

Did that mean he had feelings for Grace? Beth might have been wrong about the café. I scanned his face, seeing nothing untoward.

"Anyway," he continued, "you still need a plus one, so I'll go with you. Aren't you curious to find out why she invited you to her stately home? I know I am."

Couldn't Sam see I didn't want his company anymore? "I can report back, you know. You don't need to go to any bother," I said.

"It's a day out. Stops me getting in the way of Bruce and his mates. And I'll get to see how the other half live. I Googled Bruntney Manor, and it's amazing. A huge half-timbered Elizabethan pile."

He hadn't realised that, if his film career took off, he'd be the other half soon enough. Meanwhile, maybe he wanted to case the joint to discover what his brother could steal.

It was a bitter, unworthy thought. I scolded myself, aware that my mood hadn't been improved by a pounding headache. Sam was responsible for that. If he hadn't cheated on Beth, I'd have breezed into work fresh as a daisy this morning.

I fired one last question. "Who is she?"

Sam hesitated. His eyes darted towards the door, like a cornered animal about to break cover. "I'd rather not say."

"It's Skye, isn't it?" Rage and disgust sent a spike of agony through my temples.

Sam recoiled. "No." Collecting himself, he took a step closer to the exit.

"I hope not. She's only fourteen." I trembled, rueing the day Andrew Maxwell had first walked in for a flat white.

Sam evaded my gaze. "Actually, that's not true," he said. "She's way older."

"What?"

"She told me. We chatted a lot—"

"You don't say."

"— and Skye confided a few things."

Had I heard correctly? Arms folded, I said, "Andrew told me she was fourteen. Why would he lie?"

"Why would Andrew lie about anything?" Sam looked me in the eye now, assertiveness returning once I'd switched my focus away from him. "Come on, Jenna. He's the original sleazeball. Tell me you didn't sleep with him."

My head pulsed, fury reaching its crescendo. I was incandescent. "It's none of your business, but no."

He exhaled a long breath. "Thank God."

"You've avoiding my question by slinging mud at me."

"I didn't mean to." He held up his hands. "As far as I recall, Skye said it was all about you. Andrew didn't think you'd let her stay if you knew she was nineteen."

"But she went to school," I reminded him. "She wore a uniform."

Sam shook his head. "All a pretence."

"Why didn't you tell me? You'd complained about Andrew without good reason, but as soon as you knew he'd tricked me, you kept quiet."

"I'm so sorry." He wore a hangdog expression. "I should have said, but Skye swore me to secrecy. And, although I didn't trust Andrew, I was worried about Skye. I could at least keep an eye on her if she stayed at yours."

I was sure I was missing something. "I don't understand why she'd go to such lengths? Or risk telling you."

Sam reddened. "She liked me."

At least that made sense. Skye's attraction to Sam had been obvious. I imagined she had determined he had no interest in underage girls, and cooked up a story to get him into bed. There was no need to ask why he'd said nothing.

"As you're so close to Skye," I snapped, "can you tell me when she and Andrew are going to pay my rent?"

"You'll have to phone Andrew," he said stiffly. "I haven't heard from Skye for days. Look, I've got to dash. Bruce is bringing his van round to Montpelier to collect my stuff."

Once he'd gone, I slumped down on one of the gaily painted wooden chairs by the window. Tears flooded my eyes. Jaw grinding and head throbbing, I clenched my fists, convinced I couldn't believe a word Sam said.

# CHAPTER 24

## JENNA

Sam had dressed to impress. He stood outside a launderette on the main drag in Bedminster, looking twice as smart as everyone else. His dark suit and tie must have been purchased from a charity shop, probably in a better area. Bedminster was coming up, a trendy location for a rising star, but still rough around the edges. Sam couch-surfed in Bruce's cramped flat because he couldn't afford anything better.

I pulled up on double yellow lines. "Looking good for Grace?" I asked.

"It's a funeral." He stepped into the car and strapped himself in beside me. "You're somewhat colourful."

"She'd said it was the celebration of a life rather than mourning for the dead."

I'd organised a similar occasion for my mother, ignoring Richard's complaints about the expense. Then, I'd worn a peacock-blue skirt suit she'd bought me as a surprise gift the year before. While my style had evolved since, I still believed bright clothes brought joy. For Mitch Vincent's party, I'd chosen emerald silk with a lace collar. At a guess, it was an original fifties gown, with its nipped-in waist and flared skirt. My vintage black and white polka dot raincoat went well with it, while patent courts and a clutch bag completed the ensemble.

"I meant to say you look gorgeous," Sam said.

I flushed, politeness forcing out a curt, "Thanks."

To make it clear I wasn't interested in talking, I tuned into Radio 1 and increased the volume. The songs mingled with my memories of Sam as a seventeen-year-old, threatening a bully he'd pull her hair if she didn't let go of mine. We'd been best mates ever since. Whether smoking weed as dawn broke over the beach, on a night out, or during a busy weekend at the café, Sam had my back.

I reminded myself that the man sitting next to me, whose spicy aftershave filled the tiny Fiat, was more complicated than the rosy images I'd strung together in my mind. If we hadn't already told Grace he'd be my guest, I would have asked him to stay in Bristol.

The last couple of days had been tough. In solidarity with Beth, I wanted to fire him, but I needed Sam at the café now that trade had picked up. With less than four weeks to Christmas, Clifton was busy with shoppers, and I was taking party orders too. Sam was the perfect employee. He knew the ropes, worked hard, and had the customers eating out of his hand. Apart from statutory minimum wage increases, I'd never had to give him a pay rise. I'd struggle to replace him once he jetted off to France.

The journey dragged, especially on the long, straight stretch of motorway before we reached the Worcestershire countryside. Once we'd turned off the M5, I was occupied translating my phone's directions into the lattice of narrow lanes through which we passed.

A sign loomed ahead, announcing that Bruntney welcomed careful drivers. On each side of the road, enormous tree-lined plots hosted large detached houses. The styles were all different, from achingly modern to mock Tudor. Lawns were well-tended, gleaming SUVs sat on drives, and graffiti was conspicuous by its absence. The village had the air of a commuter suburb, clearly wealthy, but giving no clue that an ancient manor lay close by.

"Are we nearly there yet?" Sam asked.

"Let me concentrate," I snarled, glancing at the phone in its cradle on the dashboard. A straight blue line directed me to follow the main road. As I raised my eyes to the windscreen again, I noticed a roe deer dashing out in front of us. Sounding the horn and braking sharply, I managed to avoid it. It stared at us reproachfully, its features surprisingly human.

"Good save," Sam said.

"Thanks." I beamed with relief, then remembered I was cross with him. Silently, I stared ahead, pursing my lips.

Eventually, the heart of the village came into view. Properties here were older and jumbled together, front doors opening straight onto the pavement. Their half-timbering was no longer a nod to history, but the real thing. I shouldn't have doubted my GPS.

A green with a duckpond appeared by a crossroads, terraced cottages spilling around it. The phone's mechanical voice, a female reminiscent of a bossy teacher, told me to carry straight on. Shortly after I'd done so, she announced a sharp left turn.

Bruntney Manor was easy to miss. If the phone's strident tones hadn't insisted we'd arrived, I would have overlooked the entrance to the estate. It seemed merely a gap in the line of tall trees edging the road. However, it gave onto a straight track, better tarmacked than the public highway. Rows of tall limes stood guard on each side. Twenty yards into the grounds, two men in orange hi vis jackets beckoned me to halt.

I braked and wound my window down. "Hello, I'm here for the Mitchell Vincent function?" That sidestepped the issue of what to call it.

One of them held an iPad. "Your names, Miss?"

"Jenna Wyatt and Sam Farrow."

He tapped the screen. "Thank you. If you drive straight on, you might find parking by the stable block. Most likely, the yard is already full. You'll know in that case, because there will be cars stopped on the roadside." He pointed to the limes. "Just tuck yourself in behind the first one you see. All right?"

"Sure thing."

It was a quarter of a mile before I saw another vehicle, a Range Rover with the personalised plate LOG 4N.

"Hey, guess what he's called?" Sam nudged my elbow.

"I'm trying to park my car."

I left Sadie with her passenger door tight against a tree. Sam had to clamber over the driving seat once I'd exited.

"Let's find this mansion," he said.

"Not so fast." A man I assumed to be Logan jumped out of the Range Rover. He was sharp-suited, serious-looking and young, perhaps the other side of thirty from Sam and me.

He approached Sam, a cheery grin transforming him from ordinary to handsome. "Mr Farrow. I recognise you from Netflix. I'm Logan Vincent, Mitch's son and Grace's brother. How do you do?"

Having pumped Sam's hand, Logan's smile faded and his voice cooled. The hint of a sneer flickered across his face as he glanced at Sadie, then turned to me. "You must be Jenna. Welcome to our humble abode."

"Nice to meet you," I said.

"Likewise," he replied, in tones that suggested otherwise. "I'm afraid I can't stop to introduce you to everyone. A horse is in labour."

"First time I've heard that excuse," Sam said.

Eyes steely, Logan said, "I'm a vet." He climbed back into his car and powered up the engine. Winding a window down, he yelled, "Walk up the drive and you'll see the house. You can't miss it. Enjoy our hospitality."

"Grace is much more fun," Sam said. "Ready to explore?"

I minced behind him in my impractical shoes. They pinched my feet. As an insurance executive, I'd worn similar styles every day, but I was out of practice now. Luckily, we didn't have far to go. The lime avenue gave out into a huge square rose garden, surrounded on three sides by yews clipped into perfect cones. Directly opposite us, the black and white gabled manor dominated the scene. The track veered off to the right, presumably to the stable block.

A few roses still flowered in the wintry air. Their delicious fragrance drifted past as we walked across the garden's flagstone path. The day was overcast and still: the sort of weather that threatens rain but never quite manages to produce any. I was glad of the coat.

We were greeted at the door by a blast of warmth and a young woman in a navy top and trousers. She tapped at another iPad and directed us inside.

The lofty, wood-panelled entrance hall smelled of woodsmoke. Tapestries of hunting scenes hung either side of a carved stone fireplace, in which logs blazed. In a corner, a fresh-faced girl, similarly dressed, was hanging outer garments on a wheeled rack. She asked for my coat.

The spotted mac jingled alarmingly. I'd had to stuff keys and other necessities into its pockets, as my cute clutch held a phone and little else.

"Sorry," I muttered.

"No problem. Should I stick your bits in a carrier bag for you? I can put it on the same hanger."

"Sure."

"Leave it with me. Milly over there will show you to the ballroom."

We were guided to a huge, light space decorated in duck egg blue and gold. Painted trees, flowers, and cavorting couples sprawled across the ceiling, which was apparently held up by gilt cherubs at each corner. A string quartet played in front of a bay window. The music, which I vaguely recognised as Vivaldi, was almost swallowed by a murmur of conversation.

I gasped, overwhelmed by the surroundings and the sheer number of people crammed into the room. There must have been two hundred guests. Relief swept over me. Judging by the rainbow of colours, I'd chosen the right dress.

"It's something else, isn't it?" Milly said. "The fresco isn't original, but it's still part of the property's listing. I wish I had time to tell you more about Bruntney. Find me later, and I will."

A platter of champagne flutes appeared by my side. The youth carrying the tray had no chance to speak before Sam swooped upon it.

"I don't know what you're having," he joked, holding two glasses.

I removed one from his grasp, sipping the golden bubbles. A single mouthful signalled its quality. "Better start networking," I said, more breezily than I felt. The sooner I put some distance between us, the better. Sam was free to find Grace and gossip about the stars. It was obvious from Logan's reaction to us that Grace would be more interested in Sam than me.

Meanwhile, I tottered into the middle of the fray, a fixed grin on my face hiding the self-pity that engulfed me. Sam had used me as a chauffeur. I had nothing in common with anyone in this gathering of gilded strangers. Scanning the busy room, I tried in vain to make eye contact with even one of them.

"Grace!"

I turned my head to see a flurry of activity by the door. The designer, stunning in a long ice-blue number, was being mobbed. Having Googled Grace, I recognised the dress. Its Grecian pleats were Grace's signature style.

Sam, standing in front of me, waved to her. Her face lit up and she headed towards us.

His jaw dropped as she marched straight past him. So close our noses almost touched, Grace eyeballed me, gripping my arms.

"Jenna," she cried. "Oh my God. It's really you."

Automatically, I produced a polite smile. Sam had been right about Grace's exuberance. Then, as I focused on her features, my legs trembled. I'd seen online images of the designer, but nothing had prepared me for the reality of her presence. Apart from her hair, fair and straight where mine was dark and curly, it was like looking in a mirror.

# CHAPTER 25

## JENNA

Grace flung her arms around me, enveloping me in a Chanel-scented hug. Not trusting my legs to support me, I flopped against her.

"My word," Sam said. "I wish I'd listened to Martha. She said—"

"This is so exciting," Grace breathed. "I've been watching from upstairs all morning in case you were early."

"And then we were fashionably late," Sam said.

Grace ignored him. "I've always wanted a sister, and here you are. I'm sorry we had to meet like this."

"Sister?" I gasped.

The gorgeous room and glittering crowd faded from sight. My mind only had space for Grace's face, so akin to my own, and the echo of her words. Someone extracted the glass from my grip and took my arm, helping me stay on my feet. I realised it was Sam.

He stared at me, then Grace. "It might just be true. Richard isn't your dad, and—"

My brain lacked the energy to formulate a response. Breathing in Grace's perfume, I tried to make sense of what she was saying.

"—I can't believe I never noticed," Sam muttered. "To be fair, you both have such different styling."

Grace continued to blank him. Releasing me from her embrace, she asked, "Are you all right?"

I stared at her, mute, tracing my own features in the curve of her jaw and anxious blue eyes. Was I all right? I didn't think so. This couldn't be real. Nothing could have made me hallucinate, though. I recalled a party in Minehead, long ago, when I'd done mushrooms with Sam and a cat had morphed into a baby dragon. This was different. I'd merely had a single sip of champagne.

"What do you mean, 'sister'?" I asked.

"Oh my God," Grace said. "You don't know? But I thought the lawyers told you? Come on, let's get away from all these people. Follow me. We'll go to the library and I'll give you the lowdown." Gesturing to the young man hovering nearby with his tray of drinks, she added, "Could you bring a pot of tea, please, and two cups? Oh, and tissues."

If Sam noticed he wasn't being invited to join us, he didn't show it. "Lean on me," he said, placing his free arm around my shoulder. Grace carved a path through the crowd like a battleship parting the waves. We trailed in her wake.

"Hi, Jenna. I'd like to say hello." A man darted in front of us, eyes sparkling. My first thought was that Logan had returned with a personality transplant. Then I noticed the lines on his forehead and grey hair at his temples.

This must be another sibling. I had at least three, then. How was it possible? Still struggling to process the discovery, I braced myself to put on a brave face. After all, I'd projected cheeriness to my customers even when I panicked about paying my bills.

"Not now, Alex," Grace hissed.

He didn't seem put out. "Later, then. Your good health." Alex raised a glass to me.

"Our eldest brother," Grace whispered, confirming my thoughts.

She was silent as she led the way to the library, a smaller, less ornate room lined with bookshelves. It looked clean, but the still air smelled of dust. I had no sooner been seated on a comfortable old chesterfield than the youth returned, bearing a tray with a tea set and a box of Kleenex. Tactfully, he'd brought three cups and saucers.

The china was beautiful: creamy porcelain decorated with blowsy cabbage roses and gold rims. I had no doubt that it was vintage, and would have been perfect for the cupcakery.

"Milk? Sugar?" Grace asked, straining the amber liquid into all three cups and passing one to me.

My hand shook, spilling hot tea into the saucer. Sam gently took my crockery and set it on the low table in front of me.

Grace sat down. "I'm so sorry," she said. "I can't believe you didn't know that Dad—. Anyway, I only found out myself when he died."

Of course, that was why we were all here. Despite my shock, I hadn't forgotten Sam saying how upset Grace had been at her father's death. I forced myself to speak, stumbling over the words. "It must have been really hard for you."

The effort exhausted me, and I slumped back, trembling.

Tears wetted Grace's lashes. She dabbed them with a tissue. "Yes, it was awful," she admitted. "You always think your parents will live forever, and then to hear he was dead—."

I began to sob with her. Disbelief, grief and rage had once been my companions too.

119

"Jenna lost her mum nine years ago," Sam explained. He passed me the Kleenex.

Grace reached over and squeezed my hand. "God. That's terrible. I'm sorry. Should I stop talking? Would you prefer to sit quietly?"

"No." Her touch had pulled me back from the cliff-edge. Wiping away tears with my free hand, I said, "I need to hear this."

"So, Douglas was a tower of strength. He was with Dad when it happened and got him to hospital. It can't have been easy, but he phoned Mum. He helped her with everything afterwards. The funeral and all that. But he didn't tell us about you until he came round to read the will. Then he had to, really."

Sam looked askance at her. "Will?"

"Sam, I think Jenna and I should speak privately," Grace said. "Would you be a dear and give us time alone?"

My lip wobbled. "No. Please can Sam stay?" I needed a friend right now. He was the closest equivalent, whatever he'd done to Beth. I was grateful he'd insisted on coming.

There was a long pause. Finally, Grace whispered, "Okay, it's up to you, Jenna. But you didn't tell him about the will, did you, so I thought—"

"What will?" Unsettled, I drew back from her, clenching my fists to stop shaking.

Grace frowned, clearly puzzled. "Didn't Douglas tell you anything? He said he had. I mean, we only discovered you existed because Dad mentioned you in his will. And Douglas had to track you down. He told me you didn't want to see us." She blinked out tears, then added, "Sorry. I couldn't help looking for you. Having a sister was a dream come true. Then I saw you on Instagram."

"The cupcakery," Sam said.

"Your cakes are awesome." Grace was smiling again.

My tea remained untouched. I wouldn't risk spilling it again. I hugged myself, so many questions whirling in my mind that I couldn't focus.

Sam seemed to sense I needed space, "Jenna's cupcakes don't just look amazing," he said. "The taste is out of this world. You must try one. Her customers wriggle their toes and fingers with delight."

He began to demonstrate, but stopped as Grace's eyes narrowed. I remembered thinking they were having an affair. That seemed crazy now.

"I was proud of my detective work," Grace said. "You know, when Sam rang me back, I was so relieved. I thought you were the right Jenna

Wyatt, but I couldn't be totally sure until then. Another girl with the same name was in the news recently."

"No way," Sam said. "There's only one Jenna Wyatt. You checked when you set up your business, didn't you?"

I nodded. This had turned into the strangest day of my life.

"Well, it's so, so sad, but a girl called Jenna Wyatt was found drowned. It happened in Birmingham, so they reported it on local TV. Mum told me. I was devastated. I mean, imagine, we thought it was you. But when I read about the accident, the details didn't stack up. Douglas had hinted you were in your twenties, and this poor kid was only a teenager. She got blitzed and fell into a canal. Dreadful."

"Yet Jenna's here," Sam said.

"Yes, and—. Well, we look alike, don't we? It's uncanny, though. Here, see for yourself. I'll show you the news article." Removing her phone from a dinky sequined bag, Grace tapped and swiped the screen.

'Drunk and drowned,' the headline screamed above a young woman's photo.

It was Skye.

# CHAPTER 26

## JENNA

The bookshelves seemed to tilt and close in on me. I gulped. "I know that girl," I stammered.

"The other Jenna Wyatt?" Grace raised her eyebrows.

"I thought she was called Skye. Her father rented rooms in my flat." Turning to Sam for support, I noticed the colour had drained from his face. Unusually, he didn't seem able to speak.

"It can't be the same person. That's too weird. I'm getting us something stronger than tea." Grace pushed a button on a small brass bell sitting on the tea tray. A loud chime echoed through the elegant room.

I should have been elated at finding siblings, but my thoughts kept returning to the news feature. Poor Skye. While I'd resented her presence, I would never have wished her dead. I flopped back on the sofa. "Nothing makes sense."

"Too right." Another servant entered the library, and Grace requested Armagnac and three glasses.

"I'm driving," I protested weakly.

Grace's lips tightened. "Stay over. I can't host you here, although I'd love to, because my mum isn't ready for that. Someone can run you to a local hotel."

"I can't afford it."

She stiffened. "I don't believe that. You just received two million pounds, no?"

"No. Absolutely not." After a deep breath, I blurted out, "Nobody has given me money. No-one has explained our family relationship. I'm guessing, somehow, that your dad was my father too? You keep talking about Douglas, who I've never heard of. I certainly haven't met him." I wished my voice was firmer, rather than sounding shrill enough to break glass.

"Sorry, Jenna. I don't know why you weren't told, but you're right. We share the same father." Brandy arrived and Grace poured three generous tumblers, pressing one of them on me. "So, my dad had an affair with your mother. Douglas knows the full history, but he wouldn't tell me all of it. Apparently, Dad confided in him when your mother fell pregnant. They talked about divorce, but Dad didn't go through with it. My parents patched things up, and your mother married someone else."

Grace ran her hands through her shiny blonde locks, perhaps a rare sign of nerves.

"And who is this Douglas?"

"Douglas Millican is our family lawyer. Dad's best friend too. He was with Dad at the end of his life, when they went off on one of their climbing trips in Scotland. Dad had a heart attack halfway up Lurg Mhor and Douglas couldn't save him. Imagine how Douglas feels about that." A tear stole down her cheek. "As I said, Douglas read Dad's will to us. You'd been left two million pounds, as had Logan and I. None of us knew anything about you. It was nearly as much of a shock as Dad's death."

Grace had mentioned two million again. The amount seemed fantastical. It would have solved my money worries, and then some. Yet no-one had been in touch about it, whatever Grace thought. I felt awkward asking her for more information when she was so excited to have a sister.

Sam jumped in with a different question. "How did the family take the news? We met Logan earlier. I wouldn't exactly call him friendly."

I was grateful to Sam for raising the subject. While Grace and Alex had greeted me with delight, Logan hadn't rolled out a welcome mat.

Grace winced. "Logan feels sorry for Mum. She's still not coping well, but I'm sure they'll both come round. I mean, it's all Dad's fault. It's not like you're to blame, is it?"

"Right," Sam said, shifting in his seat. Maybe he realised his own behaviour wasn't perfect.

"Look, Alex and I have every sympathy for Mum. But we're thrilled to meet you. I spent my childhood pestering Mum for a little sister. And I don't begrudge you the money, by the way. Dad left us all well-provided for. I wish I'd known you before, that's all."

I risked a sip of brandy, my head beginning to clear as the coppery spirit warmed me. How many times had I wondered who my father was? Mitch Vincent had clearly been aware of my existence. He'd been in a position to track me down. Why didn't he?

Grace's eyes were moist. She gulped a slug of Armagnac. "Do you feel up to meeting Douglas? We can ask him about your inheritance. I'm sure he implied that you'd had it."

I nodded. The drink had boosted my confidence.

"Well, Douglas is here, so let's get in a huddle with him now. He's nice. And he always knows what to do." She stood up, offering me her arm.

Sam trailed after us as we made our way back to the ballroom. A babble of conversation was audible beyond its heavy oak door.

Grace opened it a crack, dramatically raising the noise level around us. She peeked through the gap. "Douglas is with my mum," she whispered. "Stay here for a second, and I'll drag him away from her. Mum needs time to get used to you. We should speak to Douglas privately, anyway."

My gaze followed the line of Grace's finger to a group by the opposite wall.

"There's Mum," she said, pointing to a woman standing with her back to us.

Mitch Vincent's widow wore a shorter version of Grace's dress, revealing a trim figure. Her honey-coloured hair was pulled back in a chignon. She was holding court to several men, one elderly and morose in appearance, the others obscured from view.

"Which is Douglas?" I asked.

"The older guy."

"The miserable one?" Sam said.

"I guess he is, these days."

"Still upset about your dad?" Sam pressed.

"Very. Also, I think he carries a torch for Mum. He doesn't approve of Andrew."

"Who is?"

"Her toy boy. Between you and me, he's fit. Would you believe she met him in church?" Grace said.

Douglas caught her eye and his doleful face broke into a smile. He waved. Grace's mother turned around. Her hand stopped mid-gesture and her lips froze. It was as if she'd turned to stone at the sight of us. When she moved again, it was to scowl and head in our direction, her clique following her.

Grace whispered, "Oops. Seems we can't avoid her. I'll keep the introductions brief." Flinging the door fully open, she swept into the ornate ballroom. Again, the crowds parted, making space for both groups to meet.

"Mum," Grace said brightly, "You must meet Jenna Wyatt. Jenna, this is my mother, Sheila Vincent, and our lawyer, Douglas Millican." She raised an eyebrow and mouthed at Douglas, "No Andrew?"

Grace's presence seemed to have perked Douglas up. He exuded amiability and expensive aftershave. Like Sam, he wore a dark suit and tie, but he'd probably spent a hundred times as much on them. They screamed designer rather than charity shop. Sotto voce, he said to Grace, "Rushed out. Something he ate."

Sheila greeted us with a deep frown. Tramlines down her cheeks hinted at a habitual expression. "I wasn't expecting this," she said to her daughter. "I'll be having words with Andrew."

"You can have them with me," Grace retorted. "I added Jenna to the guest list."

"You should have asked." Sheila glared at her.

Douglas's warmth almost compensated for Sheila's iciness. "It's lovely to meet you at last," he said, offering his hand. His grip was firm without being an endurance test. "So you're getting to know your family?"

Sheila stood back. There would be no handshake or hug from her. "I hope you haven't been telling my friends that Jenna is your sister," she hissed.

"No, Mum," Grace said. "Come on, though. They'll find out eventually, won't they?"

"Let me get you a drink, Jenna," Douglas said, as the string quartet took their places to play another piece. "Ah, Vivaldi's Four Seasons. Spring, I believe. Mitch's favourite."

"I chose the pieces he liked. And the people." Sheila glowered.

I looked down at my feet. My mother had enjoyed Vivaldi too, but it wasn't the best time to mention it.

"Douglas, can we borrow you?" Grace asked. "Jenna and I need to talk in private."

"Of course. Do excuse me, Sheila."

She looked as if she'd swallowed a wasp. Even so, Sheila was immediately surrounded by other well-wishers when Douglas left her side.

Grace led us to the door.

"Where's Sam?" I asked, a frisson of unease curling up my spine as we entered the wood-panelled corridor.

"Is that the young man who came in with you? He dashed off suddenly," Douglas said.

# CHAPTER 27

## JENNA

Sam had made a point of staying close to me since we arrived. Why would he run away? It was bizarre. A chill prickled my skin as I recalled his reaction on seeing Skye's picture. Perhaps their relationship had been closer than he'd admitted.

Douglas flashed me a sympathetic glance. "I suspect he needed the bathroom. At least one other guest had a problem. You might ask your team to stop serving the canapés, Grace."

"I'll get onto it." She tapped out a message on her phone. "Let's go to the library."

"No, we need to find Sam," I protested.

Grace grimaced. "I'm sure Douglas is right. Look, I'll ask the staff to find him and guide him back to us." She sent another message.

"He could easily get lost in this house," Douglas said. "It's a warren."

"Don't worry, Jenna. If Sam hasn't turned up when we've finished our chat with Douglas, I'll help you search for him," Grace assured me.

"Okay." My unease deepened, but I couldn't fault Grace on practicalities. I was confused and shocked, relieved that she was steering things. Douglas wasn't wrong about Bruntney Manor, either. Without Grace to lead me, I couldn't have navigated its maze of corridors.

"So," she said, when we were all seated in the library, "Douglas, Jenna tells me she hasn't received her legacy. Right, Jenna?"

I nodded.

Douglas's eyes widened. "That's not possible. I signed off the payment after Lesley Lloyd had a meeting with you, Jenna."

Still puzzled, I stood my ground. "Who's Lesley Lloyd? I haven't met anyone of that name. And how much was this payment?"

"Just north of two million pounds. The original bequest plus interest."

"I haven't had it." Both my business and personal bank accounts were overdrawn thanks to Andrew Maxwell. I wouldn't have failed to notice a deposit of two thousand pounds, let alone two million.

"As far as my firm is concerned, the cash left our client account," Douglas said. He fingered his chin. "Lesley Lloyd is my trusted right-hand woman, and I have no reason to disbelieve her. I'm so sorry, Jenna. Regrettably, I am drawn to conclude that you and I have been victims of a fraud."

Grace's mouth gaped. "Do you think the other Jenna Wyatt was involved?"

"I beg your pardon. Who is 'the other Jenna Wyatt'?" Douglas asked.

"This woman. Look." Grace swiped her phone to show him the report of Skye's death.

"Good Lord," Douglas said. "How terribly sad. I can ask Lesley if this was the person she saw. I have to say, she doesn't look anything like you."

She could mimic my moves and my voice, though. Sam had taught her to do that. With more tuition and clever makeup, Skye would have fooled a stranger like Lesley Lloyd. Had Sam worked with Skye to steal the money? His family had connections with criminals, so there was a network to help him pull off a fraud. While he didn't seem to know anything about Mitch's will, I shouldn't forget he was an actor. He was good at pretending; it was his job.

I screwed up my eyes but a tear still trickled down my cheek. Sam had used me for much more than a party invitation. Maybe I was wrong about him, though. If he'd stolen two million pounds, why would he turn up at the café afterwards, or even come to Bruntney?

Grace fiddled with her phone. "I'll call the police," she said.

"Yes," I echoed, only then twigging that I'd started to sob again. The tissues had been cleared away with the crockery and glasses. I patted my face in an effort to remove the moisture.

Douglas's voice was unctuous. "Wait a moment, Grace," he said. "I agree with you, of course. The police should be informed. But don't you think we should get our ducks in a row first, so the authorities have all the facts at their disposal? Let me investigate fully what happened at Lesley's meeting. I want a thorough understanding of the part played by my firm. Rest assured, I will leave no stone unturned."

"But it's serious," Grace said. "Shouldn't we get the police on it right away?" Still, she withdrew her finger from the screen.

"Give me a couple of hours. I'll drive straight to the office, just as soon as I've said goodbye to poor Sheila." He put a finger to his lips. "We're all on the same page, aren't we? I don't recommend sharing our suspicions. Let's hold back from troubling her."

"All right," Grace said. "Okay with that, Jenna? Let's return to the ballroom, and with luck, we'll find Sam is ahead of us."

Recalling the chattering crowd in the ballroom, I shuddered. I owed nothing to the late business magnate. Mitch Vincent hadn't cared enough to acknowledge me during his lifetime and had left a mess for Douglas to unravel on his death. I wanted out.

"Sorry Grace, I'd like to go too," I said. "I can't face the party anymore. I'll just give Sam a call."

Tempted as I was to leave him behind, maybe there was an innocent reason for his disappearance. When I rang his number, however, it went to voicemail.

Grace slipped an arm in mine. "I understand it's all too much. Look, I'll show you out. Douglas, you can come along with us, or see Mum. It's up to you."

He chose to accompany us, opening doors as I traipsed alongside her, my shoes pinching at every step. As we arrived in the entrance hall, a trio of smokers were ahead of us, sneaking out of the front door. A flash of pink caught my eye.

"That's my car! Someone's stealing it."

Beyond the perfectly spaced yew cones at the end of the rose garden, I saw Sadie, my baby pink Fiat. She executed a perfect three point turn before vanishing back down the lime avenue. My heart stopped.

"Sam," I mumbled. It had to be him. He'd seen me leave the keys with my coat.

The young cloakroom attendant glanced at me. She slipped my spotted mac off its hanger. "Is this yours, Miss? I'm afraid—"

Grace waved her away. "Not now, Courtney." She turned to me. "I'll call our security team and ask them to close the gate."

"There's a tracker on the car," I said. "It's linked to my phone, so if we can get the police out—"

Grace interrupted. "There's no time. They're miles away in Worcester." For once, she picked up her phone for a call rather than tapping out a message. As she listened to her staff, her face darkened. She finished by asking them to call 999.

"Not that it will do any good," she said. "I'm sorry, Jenna, we were too late. He got away."

# CHAPTER 28

## JENNA

Sam could go a long way with two million pounds. I didn't expect to see him, or my car, again.

"I need to get home," I told Grace. "You said your staff would ferry me to a hotel. Well, if they can take me to Worcester, I'll catch a train back to Bristol."

"I'll give you a lift," Douglas volunteered.

"Thanks, Douglas. That's sweet of you," Grace said.

"The least I can do for a damsel in distress," Douglas said.

Grace hugged me tight. "Let's meet again soon."

Courtney, the young cloakroom attendant, stepped forward. She was still clutching my mac. "I think you've got it wrong," she said.

Before I could ask what she meant, I heard yelling from the smokers outside. My mouth dropped open in shock as Sam staggered into the entrance hall. He was in a terrible state, his face bruised and his suit muddy.

"Sam, what happened?" I rushed to his side. He hadn't taken my car after all. So who had?

"Andrew Maxwell," Sam gasped, clutching his chest. "Sorry, this hurts like hell. I think I've cracked a rib. When I spotted him—"

"Here?" I gaped at him.

"What's the big deal with Andrew? He's Mum's boyfriend," Grace said.

"The toy boy?" I asked.

"Yes." She shrugged. "Do you know him?"

"He was my lodger."

Grace looked bemused.

"Let's get this straight," I said to Sam. "You saw Andrew, and didn't tell me?"

"Look, he didn't give me a chance. The second I noticed him, his eyes met mine. He recognised me. Before I could say anything, he'd legged it." Sam groaned. "I didn't want to cause a scene for you in front of your new family. I thought if I chased him—"

"But he's hurt you," I protested.

"It looks like he nearly killed you," Grace said.

"I almost had him," Sam continued. "He dived behind that coat rack – see, there, the thing on wheels – and shoved it into me. Then he obviously noticed your coat, found your car keys, and fled."

"I tried to tell them," Courtney said. "He took all your things. They were in a bag."

"I don't understand." Grace knitted her brows. "Why would Andrew steal your car?"

"Because he owes Jenna rent and wanted to give her the slip," Sam said. "Imagine his surprise when she turned up here."

"I wasn't on your mum's guest list," I said. Sheila had made that clear.

Courtney, red-faced and miserable, was fighting back tears. "I couldn't stop him," she said. "I'm sorry, Miss Wyatt."

"It must have happened so fast," Grace said gently. "Don't blame yourself. And I'm sorry I didn't listen."

The girl blushed even more furiously. "He shouted something about getting away from that psycho bitch."

Sam flinched. "I couldn't believe it, after everything you'd done for him. And everything he's done to you."

"It was brave of you to run after him," the girl said. "Him being bigger than you, and all."

Sam made a wry face. "Brave, but pointless, as he had a head start. Still, I tried."

"So how did he beat you up?" My heart thumped. A broken rib might puncture his lung. Then again, if it had, Sam wouldn't have the breath to speak.

"He didn't hit me. It was when he drove off. I hung onto the car door, because I thought I could open it and he'd stop. But he didn't, and I was flung into a tree. It fought back."

I recalled Andrew's Tesla key ring and new-smelling BMW, almost certainly hired. "He doesn't have a car, does he?" I said. Andrew could have bought one with his ill-gotten gains, though. Perhaps he'd simply arrived by taxi because he planned to drink.

"No?" Grace crooked an eyebrow. "But he's a big shot businessman. That's what Mum says."

Douglas coughed. "I fear he has fooled us all on that score."

He'd definitely fooled me. My misgivings increased. I felt sick. "Grace, has Andrew ever mentioned a daughter?" I asked.

"No. What's up? You've gone white."

Beneath his bruises, Sam had blanched too. "Are you thinking what I'm thinking?" he demanded.

I nodded. "The girl in the canal," I said. "The other Jenna Wyatt. Andrew told me she was his daughter."

"Now she's dead," Sam said. His voice was strained, the Somerset accent more pronounced than usual. "Andrew has vanished. So has two million pounds. Don't you think he has some questions to answer?"

"An audacious fraud has been perpetrated on my firm," Douglas said solemnly, "and I can only assume Andrew Maxwell is responsible."

"When he noticed Jenna and me, he'd have thought we were onto him," Sam said. "That's why he stole the car."

Grace gasped. "How awful. So, do you think he killed his own daughter? That poor girl."

"It wouldn't surprise me," Douglas said.

"You'd better to speak to the police personally, Jenna," Grace said. "I had someone call them about the car, but this is much worse. Oh my God. To think Mum loves him. I mean, she could have been next."

"Luckily, she's safe now," Douglas said. "The fellow would be mad to return here. She should step up her security to be sure, of course. Now, may I suggest that I take Jenna to the police station in Worcester?"

I nodded.

"Good idea," Grace agreed. "I'll ask someone to phone ahead and tell them you're on the way. You should call them too, Jenna, and let them know where Andrew is. Your phone can track him, no?"

"I'll come too," Sam volunteered.

"You will not." Grace pursed her lips. "You need an ambulance, and I'm calling one now. Anyway, there's no space for you in Douglas's car. It's a two-seater."

Sam's face was ashen. He wrinkled his brow, evidently realising Grace was right. "Stay strong, Jenna," he said. "And look after yourself."

"Don't worry," Douglas said. "I'll take good care of her."

# CHAPTER 29

## JENNA

Douglas had parked his scarlet sports car by the stable block. He proudly introduced it as an Audi R8 Spyder. Apparently, it would give Lewis Hamilton a run for his money. We'd get to Worcester in no time, he assured me.

"Where's Andrew?" he asked.

I showed him my phone.

"Ah, possibly heading for the M5," he said. "You told the police, did you?"

"Yes. I just gave them the co-ordinates."

"The motorway has cameras. They should catch him," Douglas said. "Hang on. Maybe he's worked that out. If he steers clear of the M5, he could slip away like a fox."

Strapping myself in, I fell silent, still trying to process the events of the past hour. With a throaty roar, the Spyder zipped around the garden, down the lime avenue, and onto the open road. The security guard appeared as a brief orange blur. I glanced at the dashboard. We were travelling at eighty miles per hour.

"You're breaking the speed limit."

"Don't panic," Douglas said cheerfully. "I know these roads."

He drove the car smoothly, but at such speed that I was glad of my seatbelt as he navigated corners. The country lanes wiggled like the ricrac braid I sewed on my bunting. At last, we reached a wider, straighter road. Douglas took the Spyder over ninety.

He glanced at me, and I realised I was chewing my lip. My nerves must be obvious.

"You really shouldn't worry," he said. "I know what I'm doing. Besides, I want Andrew Maxwell caught. He's committed an outrageous fraud on my firm, and he shouldn't get away with it."

"I don't know why he came to the party."

"He's Sheila's partner." Douglas's mouth tightened.

Remembering Grace had implied he was besotted with her mother, I felt sorry for him. "You like Sheila, don't you?" I said softly.

His jaw unclenched. "Yes, I guess it's no secret. I've known her forever. Sheila, Mitch, and I lived in Bruntney village as children. Even when I was too young to understand sexual attraction, the sight of Sheila in her school uniform was something else. Still, when we all grew up, she chose Mitch. The boy next door. I often ponder on my life, on how it might have been if she'd decided differently."

His regret was tangible. "Was Mitch your friend too?" I asked.

He nodded, clearly in the mood to unburden himself. "Yes. As boys, we did everything together. That continued as adults. We worked hard and played hard. Naturally, I was pleased for him, that he'd found the right life partner. It was my privilege to be his best man. I told Sheila I'd always be there for her too. Needless to say, it made me deeply uneasy when she became close to Andrew. A sixth sense told me he wasn't all he seemed. If only I'd known what he was capable of."

"She had a lucky escape," I said.

"Thank goodness." He brightened again. "I could reminisce about Mitch all day. Anything else you want to know about him?"

I risked the question that struck at the core of my identity. "How can you be sure I'm his daughter? Don't get me wrong, I'm delighted to find out who my father is, but how can I be certain it's Mitch?"

"Ironically, Sheila asked the same thing when I read Mitch's will to the family. I told her Mitch had been positive, and anyway, it was a named bequest so she was unlikely to succeed in overturning it."

"Did she want to?"

"I'm afraid it was her second question to me, but you shouldn't judge Sheila harshly. Your very existence came as a terrible shock to her. She's seen you today, so she can't harbour doubts. You not only resemble Mitch, but you're the spitting image of your sister, Grace."

"How did Mitch meet my mother?" I asked. Their relationship was a scab I needed to pick, but I didn't expect to like what I found. My mother had never mentioned Mitch Vincent, and she'd given Richard Wyatt's name as the father when she registered my birth. Mitch might have been a one night stand. I steeled myself for Douglas's response.

"It was through their work," he said. "She was a chocolate designer in his business. A romance developed and Mitch asked Sheila for a divorce."

"That must have been difficult for you." He'd been friends with both of them, after all.

"It was tricky," Douglas admitted. "The affair came out of left field for me, as it did for poor Sheila. I gave her a shoulder to cry on. Mitch wanted my help with the divorce, but I refused to act for either party. It wouldn't have been ethical."

I couldn't gauge how to comfort him. In spite of his slick professionalism, his voice trembled. How he must have hoped the divorce would go through and Sheila would turn to him, the boy who had admired her since their childhood.

Yet Douglas was still waiting. I supposed he'd wait forever. An old man surrounded by dusty law books, he was hardly Sheila's type. She would make the most of her looks and fortune to hook another toy boy. For Grace's sake, I prayed she'd choose more wisely than Andrew Maxwell.

After an awkward minute, Douglas pulled himself together. "Mitch decided to stay and make a go of his marriage," he said. "I gather Sheila threatened to kill herself. She didn't need to. Her outlook wouldn't have been as bleak as she imagined. There's no problem in this world that can't be solved with a dose of courage."

"I guess so," I said, unable to shake the feeling that my birth was an inconvenient accident.

Having begun talking, Douglas didn't seem minded to stop. "Mitch confessed to me that you were on the way when he made the break from your mother. For Sheila's sake, we agreed to keep it a secret. He sought to ensure you were provided for, however. He gave your mother funds to pay for your education and buy a small hotel in Minehead."

"It was a B&B." I stared out of the window, hardly clocking the countryside flashing past. Richard had enjoyed playing the successful small businessman, but he'd done little to earn a penny. Mitch had made the initial investment in the B&B and Mum and I had run it. Maybe my stepfather was reminded of his own inadequacy every time he looked at me. Still, he'd had his revenge. Any cash Richard hadn't drunk, he'd taken with him.

I blinked, deliberately dragging my thoughts from Richard by looking outside our little metal bubble. A few russet-coloured leaves shimmered in the breeze, determined to cling to their trees despite the onset of winter. Beyond, a dark ribbon of water ran at right angles to the road. We crossed the canal, seeing a houseboat chugging along. Its bright red and green paint offered a rare splash of colour in the gloomy landscape. The cheery hues did nothing to cut through my sense of dread.

The discordant sound of a Taylor Swift ringtone pulled me back into the moment.

I didn't recognise the number. "Hello?" I ventured.

"It's Grace. I just called to let you know Sam's on his way to hospital. The paramedics didn't find any broken bones, but they'll X-ray him to make sure. Are you in Worcester yet?"

"No."

"Oh." She sounded surprised. "I though Douglas would drive faster than that."

"I doubt he could be quicker."

"Never mind. If I were you, I'd phone the police to update them on Andrew's location."

"Sure," I promised her. Ending the call, I checked the Fiat's position.

"That's strange," I said to Douglas, "We don't seem near to Worcester yet, but—"

"I'm taking a shortcut," he said.

"—Andrew's really close," I finished.

"Is that a fact? Where, exactly?"

"Just past the turning for a place called Empton."

"I know. It's coming up on the left. Hold on tight." His eyes shone.

He swerved to the right, into a lane so narrow and pitted that it could have been a farm track.

Like a roller coaster, the car screeched up and down steep slopes and around blind corners. Hedges and trees suddenly loomed before us. I clutched the edges of my seat, stomach lurching.

"What are you doing? Douglas, please slow down. I want to call the police."

"No. You'll see." Douglas applied the brakes hard as a junction approached. The Spyder jolted to a halt. "Where is he now?"

Shaking, I swiped at my phone. The result stunned me. "Behind us."

"Right." With a flick of the steering wheel, we swivelled left and began racing back in the direction of Bruntney.

"Your car?" Douglas waved a finger at an oncoming blur of baby pink.

"Yes."

Douglas swung the wheel again. We were on the wrong side of the road, heading straight for my Fiat.

# CHAPTER 30

## A MAN WITH A PROBLEM

"No! What are you doing?" Jenna was screaming. He hardly noticed the words. They melded into a single, discordant shriek.

What was her problem? His car was rock solid. They would both walk away from the crash. In contrast, Andrew was toast, stuck in that pathetic piece of pink tin. The man had played into his hands, running away like that. Even so, Douglas was aware he had just one chance. He couldn't afford to let Andrew flee, vanishing like a puff of smoke until the police caught him. A clever cop would extract his secrets, for sure. Andrew knew too much.

It was a shame about the Spyder. He adored that Audi. Still, he'd claim on the insurance. No-one would imagine he'd deliberately hit the Fiat. Premiums would rise thanks to his supposed lapse of attention, but he could afford it. After paying back his debts, the remains of Jenna's legacy sat in a Panamanian bank account. That had solved one problem, he was about to stop another, and he might even rekindle Sheila's interest once Andrew was out of the picture. He'd never looked forward to an accident more.

Andrew was mere yards away, mouth wide open in horror, staring through his windscreen. Jenna's yells rose in pitch and volume. Douglas braced himself for the impact.

It didn't happen.

At the last second, the Fiat swerved, missing him by an inch. Incredulous, he slammed on his brakes. The Spyder skidded to a halt. Pumping the gas once more, he steered it to the roadside and stopped. He slumped forward, head in his hands.

For a moment, all was silent, then Jenna's voice asked tremulously, "What happened?"

"Andrew tried to kill me. He drove right at us."

"But weren't we on the wrong side of the road?"

"No, he was. Thank goodness I managed to avoid him." He'd learned that, if you lied confidently enough, people believed you.

Her narrowing eyes expressed doubt, though. "Why did you chase after him?" she asked.

"I'm sorry." His regret was real. Andrew had evaded him. "Jenna, I thought we'd help the boys in blue by tailing Andrew. We were so close. Who knows if they'll catch him now he's got away?"

"No he hasn't." She pointed out of the window, and he saw the twisted lump of metal that had once been a Fiat. Andrew had obviously lost control of the car. It had come to rest in a clump of trees on the opposite side of the carriageway.

"We'd better make sure he's all right." It was the last thing he hoped for, but sincerity was easy to fake. He'd spent decades handling difficult clients.

He jumped out of the Spyder, eager to find Andrew smashed to a pulp. Jenna followed him. She sniffed, doubtless concerned about her car.

"Help." Andrew's voice emerged from the wreck. The Fiat's door opened, hanging at a crazy angle as its driver stumbled out. You couldn't trust Italian safety engineers these days: their competence in designing crumple zones had produced a miracle.

Andrew was like Lazarus rising from the dead. He, on the other hand, saw the jaws of Hell about to open. Andrew must be neutralised at all costs, but how? He remembered his pocket knife and the nearby canal. There would be a way.

Andrew looked as if he'd done a round with Tyson Fury. He'd almost fallen out of the Fiat, but still, he had the energy to glower. "I should have known," he said.

# JENNA

Sadie would never ride again. Her cute chrome bumper and pink bonnet were mangled beyond repair. My knees buckled. The temptation to cry was overwhelming.

Incredibly, Andrew just sported cuts and bruises. His hands balled into fists, he glared at Douglas. "Did that psycho bitch send you?" he demanded.

"No." Douglas frowned. "I have no idea what you're talking about."

"She wanted me to kill you. I refused to do it." Andrew addressed me, his tone more conciliatory.

"You stole Jenna's car, though," Douglas said.

"I had to get away from the bitch. Jenna's my friend. I'd have returned it—"

"—Of course you would." Douglas infused his words with cynicism.

"You didn't need to crash into me. Extreme, wasn't it? Whatever, I'm not going back to her."

"What on earth makes you think I'd take you?" Douglas jeered.

"Who are you talking about?" I asked, terrified a fight would kick off and wishing I could defuse the tension, Hoping they wouldn't notice, I shuffled backwards.

"Sheila," Andrew said. "She tried to give me money to have you murdered."

"Impossible. Sheila's not that sort of woman." Douglas gave the impression he would kiss the ground on which she walked.

"You reckon? I'll tell you a thing or two about her," Andrew said.

They were as bad as each other. Sheila had turned them into rivals, rutting stags readying themselves for battle. I shivered.

A Range Rover drove past, braked, and did a three point turn. In my confusion, I imagined it was Logan, but as it neared, I saw the numberplate was the usual alphanumeric jumble.

Stopping next to me, a middle-aged woman wound down the driver's window. "Looks like a nasty crash. Is everyone OK?"

I was tempted to throw myself on her mercy, beg her to take me Worcester, and leave the men to fight it out. But I'd be sentencing Douglas to death. He was nearly twice Andrew's age, and he'd struggle to defend himself without my help. I couldn't desert him.

While I wavered, Andrew opened his mouth to speak. In that split-second, I thought he'd cadge a lift. It would have made sense for him to escape while he had the chance. Yet he must have had other plans, because he said, "No, we're fine." Perhaps he hoped to steal Douglas's car.

"We're fine," Douglas echoed. "Green Flag are coming out."

Her eyes darted between us all, her lips set in a grim line. Clearly, she'd clocked the friction between us and regretted stopping. It didn't take long for her to make up her mind. Before I could contradict Douglas's lie, she said, "If you're sure," and restarted her engine. The Range Rover sped off like a rocket.

"You're lucky I didn't ask her to call the cops," Douglas told Andrew.

"I'll do it now." I took out my phone.

"Don't." Douglas spoke sharply. In a more amicable tone, he said to Andrew, "We'll keep the fuzz out of it, right? I'm sure you don't want to make allegations to them about Sheila. You've got concussion. Let's get you to the side of the road. You can sit quietly and we'll work out how to get you out of this mess."

He was still trying to protect Sheila, but at what cost? I would have been happier knowing the police had our precise location. If Andrew turned violent, could Douglas and I handle him?

Douglas must have sensed my anxiety. He winked at me. "Trust me," he whispered, adding in a louder voice, "We're better off away from that car. It's a fire risk. Suppose fuel leaks out?"

"I can't smell any," Andrew said.

I sniffed the air, infused with the mould-scented dampness of autumn. There might have been a whiff of petrol. "Please, Andrew," I said.

"Safety first," Douglas urged.

Andrew seemed about to complain, then he nodded. Perhaps he smelled petrol too. Shoulders slumped, he followed Douglas, anger apparently waning. While he no longer argued with Douglas, he wouldn't look at me.

For a second, my gaze lingered over the wreckage that had been Sadie, but then I trudged after them. My impractical shoes sank into leaf mould. We skirted a thicket, ending up on a canal towpath. Reflecting the sky's dullness, the thin line of water stretched like a mirror of the road. I supposed it was just that: a secondary highway which had carried goods across the nation before trains and lorries were invented.

"The Worcester and Birmingham canal," Douglas said.

Wind ruffled the reeds lining the banks. Chilled, I stepped back from the edge.

"What's the matter, Jenna?" Douglas asked.

"I don't want to get too close."

"You're thinking about Skye, aren't you?" he said. "Don't worry, I'll keep you safe."

I stared at him. "How do you know she was called Skye?"

Surprisingly, he laughed: an unpleasant snigger. "Oh, I knew Skye very well."

If I'd been perturbed by Douglas's reaction, Andrew's was more alarming. Until then, I thought he'd calmed down. Suddenly, he sprang towards the other man, catching Douglas unawares.

"Why didn't I realise? It was you. You killed her!" Andrew screamed, delivering a punch to Douglas's jaw.

"You can't hold me responsible." Douglas shrank away from him, right hand fumbling in a trouser pocket. "You signed Skye's death warrant by involving her in your crazy scheme. It was your idea, wasn't it?"

I gasped. What did Douglas mean? I crept towards the trees, away from the water.

Roaring, Andrew rushed at the lawyer. Douglas was too near the canal, and clearly Andrew hoped to shove him into it.

I froze. Douglas and I might overpower Andrew between us. But had Douglas just confessed to killing Skye? I shouldn't have let him talk me out of calling the police. Fumbling for my phone, I checked the number of bars. There was no service, hardly surprising in the middle of nowhere.

Losing his footing, Douglas slipped. I thought he would topple into the reeds. He saved himself by throwing his body forward, reaching for Andrew's legs. Then the two men fell together onto the towpath. Andrew pummelled Douglas with both fists. He had the better of the lawyer, since Douglas hardly resisted. I inched past them.

"You took the money," Andrew panted, his face red with fury.

In spite of his plight, Douglas couldn't resist a scornful reply. "And how much did you get from Sheila? So she 'tried' to pay you, did she? No one need try where you're concerned. I bet you promised her the moon on a stick and took every penny."

"I never killed anyone," Andrew yelled, "but I'll make an exception now."

Their suits torn and muddy, the pair were no longer polished and professional, but combatants operating on some primeval instinct. Little doubting they would fight to the death, I decided to run to the road and call for help. Maybe I could flag down another motorist, or get a signal to phone the police.

Andrew sensed my movement and kicked out, tripping me. I fell. Fear forced a scream from my lips as I hurtled towards the canal. I was lucky. Despite scratching my hands on the stony ground, I landed a hair's breadth from the water. Relief surged through me.

A streak of silver flashed as Douglas's fist drove into Andrew's six-pack. At first, it wasn't obvious what had happened. Then, scrambling to my feet, I caught the sweet, metallic scent of blood. I heard Andrew grunt. Still dazed from my fall, I worked out that Douglas had used a knife.

Andrew carried on fighting. I think he'd felt the blow but didn't realise that he'd been stabbed. Suddenly, he noticed the wound. His abdomen was bleeding, an ugly stain spreading across his white shirt.

He struggled to escape, strength visibly fading. Shakily, he stood up, clutching his side as if he had a stitch. "Help me," he groaned, face twisted with pain.

I was paralysed by panic. Andrew wasn't a threat anymore. He wouldn't be murdering anyone, if indeed he was a killer at all. But how could I stop him dying?

"I'll call an ambulance," I stuttered. In that moment, I registered the red slime leaking through his fingers and dripping onto his trousers. The medics would arrive too late.

"Do you have a first aid kit in your car?" I asked Douglas.

"No." Wincing, he eased himself off the ground and staggered a few yards away. It was obvious he wouldn't help.

My skills were basic at best, but they alone stood between Andrew and the grave. I looked around for a tourniquet to staunch the flow. How I wished I'd brought even one of the vintage scarves folded neatly in my wardrobe. My tights would have to do. They were thick, black and velvety, the style I wore all winter, and long enough to wind around Andrew's cut. I dropped my bag on the ground and slipped off my court shoes.

Douglas stumbled towards us, his features bruised and swollen. The blade glinted in his hand.

"No, Douglas." Clinging to the hope that he'd only been fighting to survive, I added, "Let me bind his injury and phone for an ambulance. Even if the police come too, I'm sure we can keep Sheila out of it. Who would believe Andrew's word against hers?"

"It's too late. He tried to kill me, to throw me in the canal. You saw, Jenna." Douglas's puffy eyes bored into me. "Well, we'll see how he likes a taste of his own medicine."

I was still removing my tights when Douglas shoved the swaying Andrew, hard, into the reed bed.

The vegetation slowed his fall but couldn't stop it entirely. Andrew screamed, a wail combining pain and fear. He clutched at the reeds. In summer, when they'd been green and alive, he might have stood a chance. Now, they were brittle brown sticks. They broke as soon as he put weight on them. With a splash, the depths claimed his lower body.

"I can't swim," he shouted, arms flailing, hands stretching for the bank.

"Just try to float," I yelled. Finally freeing my tights, I tried to throw one black nylon leg towards him. Limp, it fluttered in the breeze. I had a second go, looping the other leg around a fist and bracing myself.

"Drop that. He isn't worth it." Douglas brandished his knife. Then he placed it at my throat.

# CHAPTER 31

# JENNA

I didn't argue, not daring to utter a sound as I relaxed my grip on the tights. Andrew's gaze fixed mine, and I retched, sick with fear and guilt. His brown eyes bulged in terror. He knew he was going to die.

The reed bed must have been shallow, because he wasn't submerged right away. For a moment, he stood, swaying, head and torso above the water. Then he lost his footing. With a scream, arms flailing, he vanished below the surface.

I shivered, goosebumps prickling my bare legs and feet. The cold metal pressed into my throat. "Please let me go," I begged, a tear stealing down my cheek.

"If you don't do anything stupid." Douglas looked meaningfully at the canal.

"I won't," I promised, following his gaze, and wishing I hadn't. Andrew's body bobbed, face down, in the rippling water by the reeds.

Douglas removed the knife from my neck. It was a short blade, but I'd already seen evidence of its deadliness. He was skilled enough in its use. How many others had he killed? I had no illusions about Skye's death now.

Stepping back, he appraised my exposed legs. "I haven't decided what to do with you yet," he said conversationally. "I generally go for women somewhat younger than you."

What made him think any female would find him attractive? I gagged. Over twice my age, Douglas didn't do it for me. It wasn't a smart move to tell him, though.

"I thought you liked Sheila," I asked. Perhaps if I kept him talking, help would arrive. Passers-by might see the wrecked vehicles and stop to investigate. I'd spoken to the police earlier and given them the general direction of Andrew's journey. It would be enough for them to find us, wouldn't it? I prayed they'd be in time.

Douglas twisted his split lip into a grimace. "I wasn't entirely honest with you," he admitted. "Sheila has been a disappointment to me. As a teenager, she was magnificent. Once she'd married Mitch, I'd already lost interest, although I dallied with her. She was convenient."

"This was before he died?" I asked, swallowing another wave of revulsion. Douglas had claimed Mitch was his best friend.

144

"On and off," he said casually. "Mitch never suspected, so what's the harm? It suited both me and Sheila to be careful. She enjoyed a taste of forbidden fruit. And that's all I was, if I had but realised. I assumed we'd get together when Mitch died, and my money worries would be over. The last thing I expected was Andrew Maxwell." He glared at the reed bed, where his rival's body floated amid the dying vegetation.

Gut churning, I tasted bile. The dark intuition that had gripped me wouldn't disappear. He was more of a monster than I'd imagined. "What exactly happened when you and Mitch were up that mountain?" I asked.

"Lurg Mhor?" Douglas said. "It was terribly sad. Mitch overdid it and went into cardiac arrest, as I told you."

"How quickly did you call the emergency services?" I demanded.

"What are you implying?" Douglas laughed. "Aren't you a clever girl? Chip off the old block. I may have waited a while, I suppose."

Instinctively, I recoiled at his amusement, which merely increased it. His eyes twinkled with glee.

"It seemed a gift from the gods at the time," he said cheerily.

My phone rang, its vibration causing my bag to rattle on the path where I'd dropped it. I finally had a signal, not that it was any use now.

"Don't move," Douglas said.

"Of course not." The chirpy sound was disconcerting when a devil stood in front of me. Thankfully, it stopped. I smiled at Douglas. My mind raced, trying to work out how to keep him talking. "A piece of luck for you," I said. "The perfect crime. Or was it even a crime?"

"Oh yes, under both English and Scots law." He chuckled.

I cursed myself for asking that question. With his latest revelation, we'd passed the point of no return. He couldn't allow me to leave this spot alive. Yet he didn't seem in a hurry to finish the conversation.

I nearly choked on a mouthful of vomit. Gulping it back, I softened my voice. "It must have been awful for you when Sheila turned to Andrew Maxwell."

Douglas's nostrils flared, all merriment extinguished. Once more, he squinted at the body gently resting on the canal's surface. Evidently satisfied, he appeared to relax. "Yes, well. Sheila was totally taken in by that charlatan," he said bitterly. "Maxwell is a conman with a record as long as your arm. He approached her at her local church – did you hear that? His MO is pretending to be a successful businessman. He's well known for it."

Douglas was even better at faking it. None of the Vincents had guessed he was a murderer. I didn't think he'd realised the irony.

"How did you find out so much about Andrew?" I asked.

"My firm often runs checks on individuals. We have to do it to comply with professional rules, or, as in your case, to pay out a legacy. My team slipped up there, I'll admit." He tutted.

"Weren't you—," I struggled for the words, aware he could stab me without blinking, "working with Andrew on that?"

"Collaborate with that jailbird?" he sneered. "You should have known better than to trust him. For twenty pounds, you would have uncovered enough information on Andrew Maxwell to send you running for the hills. Instead, you rented a flat to him without taking the most basic of precautions. Really, you should be more careful."

"Andrew was persuasive," I admitted. "He came across as desperate for a place to live with Skye. His daughter."

"Are you serious? Skye wasn't his daughter. I believe the 'woke' term is a sex worker." He made air quotes with his fingers.

Surely he was lying? I gawped at him. "But she was so young."

Douglas leered. "That's the point, isn't it?"

When Sam had claimed Skye was older than fourteen, I'd dismissed the notion. What an idiot I'd been. A grim suspicion began to form. "How exactly did you know Skye?"

"In the biblical sense, as it were. And you've presumably deduced that Andrew did too."

Sam had said Skye didn't attend school. At last, I believed him. It was obvious what she'd been doing with her time. Her baby's father had been hiding in plain sight.

Douglas looked me up and down, his gaze calculating. At any minute, he would pitch me into the canal.

Desperate to distract him, I said, "I had no idea Skye was anything but a schoolgirl, and that Andrew wasn't her doting father. It still confuses me when I try to guess who they were and what they did. Yet you worked it out. How?"

A smile flickered on his lips. "Well now. They had a clever plan. It must have been Andrew's doing because Skye didn't have two brain cells to rub together. Nice legs, though. I remember them splayed across my desk."

He glanced at mine. I swallowed, resisting the urge to be sick.

"So," Douglas said, "Skye and I had fun together. We did things you wouldn't believe. There was the swingers' party and the hot air balloon… Anyhow, while I once entertained the notion that she harboured affection for me, I'm afraid actions speak louder than words. I accept now that her intentions were strictly business. My belief is that she copied documents in my office. Not that I lacked care, as such, but if I popped out for a minute, she'd have had access to papers on my desk."

"And then?" I asked. "How would that lead to two million pounds vanishing into thin air?"

"It didn't, to begin with. My guess is she started by selling information to Andrew. That would be how he discovered Sheila had been widowed and left in comfortable circumstances."

"And arranged to meet her in church."

"Exactly, so her guard would be lowered. She'd be less likely to question his lies."

"But you didn't take him at face value. You investigated his background. So why didn't you go straight to Sheila?"

Douglas shook his head. "Why indeed? Don't forget, Andrew swept Sheila off her feet. A woman in love won't listen to bad news. Sheila would have made excuses for him and told me I was jealous."

Was that how I'd behaved when Sam expressed doubts about Andrew? If only I'd listened. We'd all been wrong about Douglas, however, the thief and killer masquerading as a boring family lawyer.

"Appearances are everything to Sheila," Douglas said. "It's her blind spot. She was upset, not just by your existence, but the fact that it was out in the open. Mitch's will is publicly available if you know where to look. I'm sure Andrew got his hands on it.

"It demonstrated a fault-line in her apparently perfect marriage, and she'd been so careful to keep her liaison with me secret. She may well have offered Andrew cash to arrange a hit. As it happens, she even asked me. I declined."

"Thank you," I said. "But you told Andrew earlier that she wasn't that kind of woman."

"I lied. But I can assure you that I'm not a gun for hire, and won't be treated like one. I deserve more than that from her. My guess is that Andrew thought the same. Laughable, isn't it?"

"So?" I'd aimed to keep him talking, but the more he revealed, the more puzzled I became. Almost forgetting the danger he posed, I was riveted.

"Andrew saw that you would inherit a substantial amount. He arranged for Skye to change her name by deed poll. I found out last week that she'd done so, but not before she'd fooled Lesley Lloyd." Douglas sniggered. "Poor Lesley, so prim, proper, and eager to please. She'll be mortified once she learns she met an imposter."

"I don't understand. Why would Skye go to the trouble of changing her name?"

"It would be a red flag if my firm was asked to pay funds to someone else's bank account. With a deed poll certificate, Skye could simply tell her bank to change the account details. Of course, Millican Syme needed to make further checks, but I understood from Lesley that they stacked up. Skye brought proof of identity and address. I assume Andrew forged them."

I recalled Skye's geography homework: how she'd asked to see my passport. Would I find it in the drawer if, somehow, I escaped with my life? I had a hunch it would be missing. "She stole them from my flat," I said.

Douglas whistled. "Quite likely. And that would be where she got her hands on my letter to you, too. It explains why I wrote to you about Mitch's bequest, but you didn't know."

"Do you think," I asked, voice trembling as the last piece of the jigsaw fell into place, "that they rented rooms so they could intercept that letter? Would Skye have known you'd write to me?"

"She might easily have got wind of it. I made a mistake in trusting Skye in my office, didn't I?" He smirked, visibly revelling in the memory. "At least I came to my senses when Andrew Maxwell tried to lure me to a meeting in Scotland."

"How do you mean?"

"They knew I'd recognise Skye, so they needed me out of the way when she visited Millican Syme. She arranged an appointment. Then Andrew, purporting to be Gordon Smith, a Scottish financier, requested a meeting with me in Edinburgh at the same time. He emailed my PA with a convincing story of a corporate takeover and a tasty fee. She agreed. I can't criticise her. It was far more important for me to bring in new business than to meet you personally. Lesley could be trusted to do that."

It showed how far Andrew would go to steal two million pounds. He must have thought it was worth it. It hadn't done him or Skye any good in the end, because Douglas was prepared to go further. How long before he lost patience with me? I asked, "You said Andrew tried to lure you to Edinburgh. So he didn't succeed?"

"I wasn't born yesterday. When I phoned the company Gordon Smith ostensibly worked for, they hadn't heard of him. His LinkedIn profile was a pack of lies. It was an obvious attempt to draw me away from my office. My PA and I pretended I was travelling to Scotland – she'd prepared excuses about traffic accidents should this Gordon Smith phone her – but I stayed in Birmingham. It was plain to me that we'd have an interesting visitor. Then, as I sat watching our CCTV, Skye arrived."

"You could have stopped her."

"Why would I do that?" He seemed genuinely surprised. "I'd made some unfortunate investments – Chinese property, and so on – and there were loans to repay. I needed cash. Desperately. Here was a chance to get it, handed on a plate. I authorised the payment. All I had to do afterwards was persuade Skye to give me the money before Andrew could take it from her. Which, incidentally, I'm sure he intended to do."

I didn't ask how he'd persuaded Skye. The details were probably more than I could stomach. "You said you needed cash," I ventured. "Can we cut a deal?"

"But why should I? Haven't you forgotten something?" He gazed at his knife, then at my face, his eyes piercing. "It really is a shame, you know. I see Mitch in you, Jenna. He would have been so proud of you."

I heard the blare of sirens, rapidly increasing in volume. Douglas's mouth twitched. "Time to go," he said. "I will be the star witness in your inquest. A terribly sad affair. I saw you and Andrew fighting and couldn't stop you both falling in."

He was going to use the knife. If I let him, I was dead. Injured, I'd have no hope of swimming to the opposite bank.

I had one chance of survival. With no time to hesitate, I spread out my arms and legs, flinging myself backwards into the reeds.

The vegetation slowed my fall. So did something larger and more solid. I tried not to think about it. Skin tingling at the icy water's assault, I sneezed as a massive splash sent spray up my nostrils. I prayed my head would stay above the surface.

I'd been raised by the sea. Everyone knew the danger of cold water, how swimming was impossible on impact. Even if Andrew had been an Olympic champion, he couldn't have saved himself. Within seconds, his body would have gone into shock. He'd hyperventilated, drawing water into his lungs.

149

If I took in air with that first unconscious gasp, I might live.

My clothes flapped around me, helping me float. With the last of my strength, I kicked out at the reeds.

As my limbs numbed and dizziness overwhelmed me, a curious peace descended. Slipping into darkness, I caught a glimpse of blue light, and inexplicable flashes of red and green. The sound of sirens faded. Nothing mattered anymore.

# CHAPTER 32

## JENNA

"Jenna?"

"She's sleeping."

The two voices, one male and one female, wormed their way through my subconscious. The man sounded familiar, and not in a good way. My eyes flicked open.

The pair loomed above me: a nurse, brown curls tied back in a ponytail, and Richard Wyatt. My stepfather's bushy hair was greyer and his widow's peak more pronounced than a decade ago, but it was unmistakeably him. He wore the same clothing he'd always liked: jeans, an Aran jumper, and a parka.

"Hello, Richard," I said. My faltering words echoed through brain fog.

He shuffled awkwardly next to the bed. "I brought you grapes," he said, flourishing a bunch. "That's what you do for hospital patients, isn't it?"

"I'll find a bowl for them," the nurse said. "Don't forget, Mr Wyatt, just ten minutes. Jenna needs to rest." She tugged at the blue curtain which created a cubicle around us. A gap appeared, through which she slipped away.

Richard settled himself on a moulded plastic chair next to the bed, leaning forward to look at me. His brown eyes were baggier than I remembered. "How are you?" he asked, his Somerset lilt more sympathetic than I'd expected.

"Fine, I think. They say I can go home tomorrow."

"Do you need a lift? I can take you. They said you're in Bristol now. Well, I've come up from Cornwall, so it's on the way back."

"I'll get a train." Under the covers, I pinched a fleshy thigh. The pain proved I wasn't dreaming. Richard was real enough, but I didn't want transport or anything else from him.

"Why are you here?" I asked, wondering if he needed money. He'd be disappointed to find Mitch's legacy had vanished.

"The police contacted me to say you had an accident." His lip quivered. "I feared the worst, after what happened to your mum."

"Yet here I am."

"Thank goodness," Richard said fervently. He pushed back a lock of hair. "What happened?"

"Cold water shock. I fell into a canal."

"The coppers said it was more than that. You were pushed."

"Sort of." I yawned, lids drooping as I fought the urge to sleep.

Fatigue made it hard to concentrate, but my memory was returning. At first, I'd recalled vignettes, nothing more: a knife flashing as I jumped, the icy chill of black water, and strong hands hauling me onto a boat. Eventually, I'd recovered enough to give a statement to the police. They'd been alerted by the woman in the Range Rover, who had also called an ambulance. It was too late for Andrew, of course, but I'd been whisked to hospital. So had Douglas, although he was taken into custody later. I was safe.

Opening my eyes fully, I peered at Richard.

"I'm glad I didn't lose you," he said.

He'd lost me eight years ago. I wished he'd leave me alone, but I should be polite. He'd brought grapes and been worried enough to travel to a hospital in Worcestershire. He'd mentioned Cornwall, hadn't he? "I thought you lived in Turkey," I said.

"I came back when I met Gail. She saved my life."

Despite my antipathy towards him, I was intrigued. "Want to tell me about it?" I asked.

Richard hesitated, lips tightening. Finally, he said. "I'm an alcoholic. I don't suppose you knew?"

"I worked it out. There were clues." Receipts for his trips to the cash and carry always included purchases of alcohol, manifesting later as empty bottles left out for recycling. Then there were the pub lunches which stretched to midnight.

I'd been well aware of his addiction, and so had Mum.

He half-smiled. "Kids aren't thick, are they? Anyway, I wanted to put all that behind me, make a fresh start. That's what I hoped for when I moved to Turkey. But the voice in my head went with me. You know, the constant nagging that you're not good enough?"

"It's your subconscious," I said.

He stiffened. "It sounded more like your mother."

I chewed the corner of my lip in an effort to stay silent. For most of my life, his scolding had echoed inside my head. I was stupid, I was idling, I should serve that table now. Why play the blame game, though?

"She made me feel second best," Richard said.

"To Mitch?"

He twisted his face. "So you know? She was nothing to him. Nothing," he repeated bitterly. "He bought his way out of trouble, like those people always do. Utterly ruthless."

"He was my father." My defence was half-hearted. I'd already formed a similar opinion of Mitchell Vincent.

"Yes, and you're the spit of the man. I'm sorry. I couldn't get over that." His grim tone softened. "I'm more chilled around kids now. Gail and I have a little girl, eighteen months old. Do you want to see a picture?"

"Sure."

He took out a phone, an old and scratched Samsung, and showed me a photo. A strawberry blonde cherub beamed at me.

"This is Willow. She doesn't look much like me. I guess that's a mercy for her."

"Maybe the hair," I said. "Yours was sandy before—"

"— before I got old," he finished. "I'm lucky to have made it, considering I was drinking myself to death. Fortunately, I bumped into Gail outside a bar. She'd stayed at our B&B as a teenager. Can you believe that?"

"I don't recall. So many customers. There wouldn't have been much for her in Minehead."

"She loved it. Even then, she was into yoga, taking her mat to the beach. That's what she does now in Cornwall, running classes and retreats."

He had switched on a dim memory, of a thin and supple girl doing exercises in our garden as the sun rose. She seemed an adult to me; I must have been a small child then. Same old, same old, I thought. Richard had attracted a hard-working partner and was sponging off her.

"I do supermarket deliveries," he said. "Running a business is too stressful for me, but this way, I can share childcare. I fit my shifts around Gail's classes." He paused. "I've surprised you."

"It's a big change."

He nodded. "Well, I don't drink. Daren't. Just one, and it's down the slippery slope again. But if I'm honest, I don't need to. Family life suits me. And that leads me to say that I regret not living up to my obligations when you were younger. You weren't mine, but I knew your mum was pregnant with you when I married her. I should have made more of an effort. Can we start again, Jenna?"

153

I studied his face, as if seeing him for the first time. Richard would have been twenty-five when I was born. Whatever promises he and my mother had made to each other, it would have been a big deal to begin a business, marriage, and parenthood almost simultaneously. He'd matured and learned from his mistakes, but did I care?

I steeled myself. Richard was doubtless just using the superficial charm he'd developed for customers. At any moment, he'd ask for money.

"Please?" Richard pressed.

"I'll think about it."

"I'm glad you didn't say no." He folded his arms. "There's one more thing. When I liquidated the B&B, I took everything. But you'd contributed to its success. I guess Mitchell Vincent did too." He said the name with distaste. "Gail and I aren't rich like him, but if you're struggling, let us know. We'd be happy to help."

"Gail agrees on that, does she?"

"Her idea. And she's right." He chuckled. "She's annoying like that."

I blinked, unsure how far to test him. Did I even want to?

Then I thought about the café, sinking in a mire of debt. Mitch's bequest wouldn't arrive in time to pay my mortgage, if it ever turned up. The police had said it could take months or years to trace it. Once Sam flew away to start filming, I wouldn't have to pay his wages, but I'd be swamped with work. The party deliveries, cash and carry trips and occasional networking would be squeezed into the evenings, when buses were unreliable and taxis expensive. I needed Sadie more than ever. Yet Sadie was gone.

"My car was written off in the, er, incident," I said. "It was small and really old, but I rely on it."

Richard tapped his nose. "I'll see what I can do. Friends in the motor trade, you know? I'm guessing at a little runabout, low insurance group?"

The nurse returned without a bowl for the grapes. "It's been twenty minutes, Mr Wyatt."

He stood up and stretched. "Okay, I'm going. Take care of yourself, Jenna, all right?"

He stroked my hair. I'd forgotten how he used to do that when I was a child. As the nurse held the curtain for his departure, I reflected that memories were selective.

# CHAPTER 33

## JENNA – THREE MONTHS LATER

"Hello sis." Waving from the doorway, Grace stepped over the café's threshold.

I'd last seen her three months ago, just before I was discharged from hospital. She'd brought chocolates and charmed the nurses, but she'd been incredulous when I mentioned Sheila had wanted me killed. I feared I'd lost her friendship. Yet here she was, bringing her commanding presence to Clifton. Although she wore jeans rather than one of her glamorous creations, all eyes were upon her. Martha's and Kimberley's nearly popped out of their sockets. Then, as Grace made her way to the counter, they spotted her companion.

"Sam!" Kimberley shrieked with excitement. "You're back."

I craned my neck to see past Grace, catching a glimpse of tanned skin and a leather jacket. Was it really Sam? He was supposed to be on a film set. Last night, he'd even texted to wish me sweet dreams from the south of France.

"I missed you, Kimberley, my love." There was no mistaking his Somerset tones for anyone else. He held out his arms, embracing Kimberley when she rose to her feet.

Now I had a better view, I gasped in surprise. He'd cut his hair short. It suited him.

He beamed at me over Kimberley's shoulder. "I'll introduce you to my friend, Grace, in a minute," he told her.

"Special friend?" Martha asked.

"A gentleman never tells," Sam replied.

My other patrons were agog. Celebrity-spotting was something of a sport in Clifton Village, but not at the cupcakery after he left. Lauren, who had his old job, seized the moment. Her upselling skills even beat Sam's. Flitting from table to table, she asked the customers if they'd like anything else.

"I didn't expect to see you this weekend, especially together. It's been ages." I smiled at the visitors, my heart lightening. Sam's absence had left an unexpected hole in my life. Since I'd first met him, we'd socialised regularly. That hadn't stopped during the pandemic, when he'd cycled to Clifton to join me for socially distanced walks. Then, after Christmas,

Sam had jetted off to France. We'd phoned each other, but it hadn't been the same.

Grace air-kissed me. "Sam had a break in filming, so we thought we'd pop in. Because you're worth it," she said.

I glowed. It was a sign of reconciliation as well as a compliment.

Sam finished accepting greetings and joined Grace in front of me.

"You didn't say you were coming," I berated him.

"I wanted to surprise you. Sorry, I'd forgotten how busy you were on Saturdays."

"And the rest of the week. The oxygen of publicity." That would only increase when Douglas's trial was over. I had newspaper deals lined up. They'd pay off my second mortgage. Meanwhile, financial pressures had eased. I pointed to the new furniture I'd shoehorned into a corner. "Remember I told you we had four extra covers? Takeout orders have gone stratospheric as well."

"It's such fun here," Lauren said. "Never dull."

Sam hugged her too. She was one of his resting actor buddies, a redhead who adored vintage clothes as much as I did.

"How's the film going?" I asked over the hiss of the espresso machine.

"Two weeks left, then it's a wrap," Sam said. "But guess what? I've been offered another role starting next month. Shooting in Bath. How good is that?"

"It'll be huge." Grace clutched his arm. "I'm so thrilled for you."

"Who else is in it?" I asked.

Sam made a zipping motion across his lips. "I'm not allowed to say. If I thought Grace would spill the beans, I'd kill her."

"I'm very scared." Grace's eyes sparkled.

"That's enough about me," Sam said. "You're looking well. Is the Douglas situation sorted yet?"

"No, he's still pleading not guilty. It means there will be a trial. The police say they have a strong case, though."

I fell silent, unwilling to say more in front of customers eager for titbits. Douglas had admitted a great deal to me beside the canal, but he'd denied it all when the police caught up with him. Mitch Vincent had died of natural causes, he told them. Didn't the death certificate say so? Then, he'd been forced to kill Andrew in self-defence, while my plunge into the canal arose from a misunderstanding. Skye's murder was nothing to do with him; he claimed Andrew was responsible, having been paid by Sheila to do away with Jenna Wyatt.

I reckoned he was lying. So did the police, who were painstakingly checking bank transfers, CCTV, and mobile phone records. They'd already discovered Andrew was heading for a chop shop on the outskirts of Birmingham, presumably to get what little he could for my car. What would he have done next? I didn't think he would have returned to kill me, although I was prepared to believe he'd taken money from Sheila for it.

I shuddered. Like Sam's, my cuts and bruises had healed. However, I hadn't lost the memory of dark, deadly water.

"Come on," Sam said. "It's over now."

Grace shook her head. "Some things stay with you. I always thought Andrew was too good to be true, but I didn't suspect old Douglas. Nor did Mum. She is absolutely shell-shocked. I mean, she's questioning her taste in men, put it that way."

Despite Sheila's hostility towards me, I sympathised. Ned had been unbelievably callous. If I'd followed my instincts and jumped into Andrew's arms afterwards, I'd have fled straight from frying pan to fire.

Grace stretched to touch my shoulder, nearly receiving a blast of steam from the coffee machine. "Mum's angry with Dad too. And I am, a bit. He shouldn't have kept you secret until his death. Whatever Mum thinks, I want us to be friends. How about it, Jenna?"

"The answer is yes." I finished making a drink, then eased my way around the counter. Hugging her, I added. "Much more than that, sister."

Grace glowed. "We've got so much catching up to do."

Sam coughed. "Jenna, are you free for cocktails tonight?"

"That's another easy question." I grinned. "As it happens, I am. I'll see you both later."

"Not me." Grace exchanged a glance with Sam. "I'm catching up with a couple of besties this evening. But I'm staying in Bristol, so how about brunch tomorrow?"

"It's a shame, but I can't. I was planning to come to the café rather than leave Lauren on her own. Why don't you pop in for a cupcake instead? I'll make all Sam's favourites."

Were my eyes playing tricks, or did he wink at her?

Grace chuckled. "Sam told me you'd say that."

After promising premiere tickets to Kimberley and Martha, they left, chatting merrily. My gaze lingered on the door long afterwards. Sam had evidently been keen on Grace since they first met. He was happy at last, so why wasn't I?

Sam was waiting for me as I locked up. We didn't go to the Ivy. The upscale venue was a special place for Beth; it would have felt like a betrayal to drink there without her. Anyway, for a Saturday night, we'd have had to book a week ago.

There were two other cocktail lounges in Clifton Village, one brash and neon-lit with a feminine vibe, and the other dark and intimate. I let Sam choose. He opted for the latter, to my lack of surprise.

"My treat," he offered, once we'd been seated across a petite table from each other. He inspected the cocktail menu. "I'm having The Last Word."

It was the signature drink, named after the bar: a bright green liquid served in the standard conical glass.

"Your good health." He gulped half of it after the toast, almost spilling the remainder when he replaced his glass on the table.

"You're supposed to sip it," I said, demonstrating with a retro Singapore Sling.

"Sorry. A long day." Sam knocked back the rest and ordered more.

A tea light flickered in the space between us. The alcohol warmed my veins. I began to recover from another intense Saturday. Although I'd moved to Clifton for places like this, it was a rare pleasure to relax in one. "Where are you staying?" I asked. "I guess Grace is accustomed to the best."

"Oh yes." He grinned. "She booked into the Avon Gorge Hotel, but—"

"That's a stone's throw from my flat," I interrupted. "You could both come to my place for breakfast."

He paused, appearing to consider it. "Let's see how blitzed you get before asking Grace. Having the same again?"

"Please."

In the café earlier, he hadn't displayed his usual nervy, wired edge. It was back now, although he slowed down his boozing when fresh drinks arrived. "Any news on your legacy?" he asked.

I sighed. "No sign of it yet. It's with Millican Syme's insurers. The police haven't tracked down the funds, but it seems Douglas had major financial difficulties. He'd borrowed money from the sort of lenders who collect it by breaking legs."

I recalled that Sam had a cousin in the trade, and changed the subject. "To be honest, I don't care whether I get my father's cash or not. Remember all the trouble it caused? Douglas killed for it. Skye and Andrew died for it, and I almost did too. Richard nearly drank himself to death with his share. It's not as if I've earned a single penny, either. I feel like a lottery winner who didn't even buy a ticket."

"Talking of earnings, how's business?"

"Good. Better than that, it's amazing. And I found a brilliant flatmate through Gumtree, a personal trainer. I don't need Mitch's blood money."

Douglas had said he saw Mitch in me. I might resemble my father in appearance, but in character, I favoured my mum. My goal was to make people happy.

Sam rose to his feet, crept around the table, and knelt down. He hugged me tight. "I'm glad you take that view. Maybe if they pay out your two million pounds, you could give some to the foodbank or another charity helping folk who are struggling."

"All of it," I said boldly. "I'm not keeping a penny." I snuggled into him, enjoying the moment. Being in his arms was more pleasurable than I expected. The memory of our drunken student kiss floated into my mind. I pulled away. Was I crazy? At a stroke, I could ruin both my oldest friendship and my newest, the fledgling connection with my half-sister. Anyway, Sam was a player. I still didn't know if he'd slept with Skye. She'd been using him to find out about me, clearly, but how far had she gone?

"Did I do something wrong?" Sam eased himself back into his chair. He took a swig of the lurid cocktail. The soft lighting cast a long shadow on his face.

He didn't make eye contact as I glanced over at him. Was he sulking? I felt a rush of annoyance at his self-pity.

"Beth is okay, seeing as you ask," I said.

"Good." He fidgeted.

Was that all he had to say about her? "No thanks to you," I pointed out. The Singapore Slings fuelled my indignation. These days, I was so busy, and my flatmate so health-conscious, that I rarely drank. The alcohol had gone straight to my head, mingling in a toxic brew with my sympathy for Beth.

"I never meant to hurt her."

"Well, she's so over you," I said waspishly, although a nagging doubt told me she wasn't. "In fact, she got engaged to her boss last week."

"What?"

I knew that would grab his attention. "They got together at the office Christmas party."

"It's sudden, that's all."

"Talking of sudden, you dumped your crush quickly," I said.

"What do you mean?"

"You told Beth you were in love, but not with her. Remember? You admitted it to me."

I pressed on. "Whoever your girlfriend was, it couldn't have been Grace. If Grace was your lover, you wouldn't have had to go to the party in Bruntney to meet her again." Glaring at him, I was nevertheless impressed by my powers of deduction. Sherlock Holmes had nothing on me.

"I told you," Sam muttered, "I went to Bruntney because I thought you needed company."

I was on a roll. "Anyway," I finished triumphantly, "like I said, once you'd hooked up with Grace, it didn't take you long to get over the other girl."

"I'm not over her," Sam said.

"Oh? I suppose you're going to break Grace's heart next?"

Sam stared at me with an expression I hadn't seen before: a mixture of regret and longing. "You think Grace and I are a couple?" he said. "No. My heart lies elsewhere."

"Where then?" I challenged him.

"Don't you know?" he said softly.

It wasn't Skye. How could I ever have imagined it? The truth lay in his eyes. It had been right in front of me for years.

Lightness welled up within me. "Why didn't you say?" I asked.

He reddened. "It was never the right moment. There was always a rich boyfriend on the scene."

"You make it sound like I chased them for their money," I murmured, too elated to take offence.

Sam shook his head. "No, they chased you. It was obvious you were out of my league. What could I offer you?" He paused. "Once, when you'd just chucked that idiot with the blue sports car, I worked up the courage to tell you how I felt."

I pulled a face. That was a romance I'd long consigned to oblivion. "The one before Ned," I said. "He was dreadful. I can't say you didn't warn me."

"We went to a party together," he said. "I kissed you. You probably don't even remember."

My cheeks grew hot. "How could I forget?"

"When I went to get you a drink, Ned moved in on you and started chatting you up."

I shuddered. "My biggest mistake."

"Don't blame yourself. Ned was a smooth operator. I guess he figured I wouldn't start a fight. It would have spoiled everyone's fun." Sam shifted the candle aside. He leaned forward. "We can pick up where we left off, if you like?"

Even as butterflies filled my chest, a sense of unease held me back. "I'm honestly not sure," I said, voice shaking. "I got it wrong so many times. Ned was a disaster, and as for Andrew—"

Sam froze.

"Like I told you, we didn't get involved," I said hastily, "but I trusted him. I'm not a great judge of character, you know? I shouldn't rush into anything."

Silence hung between us. Sam reached out and squeezed my hand.

A spark of electricity sent warmth surging through me. I gulped. Maybe, just maybe, I stood a chance of getting it right this time.

"Perhaps we can take it slow?" I suggested.

A smile spread across his face. "Of course," he said. "Take as long as you need."

We had to start somewhere, though. I edged towards him, heart thumping. Our lips met for the second time.

oooOooo

**He stole her childhood. Can she escape before he takes her life?**

**BRIGHT LIES** is AA Abbott's darkest psychological thriller. Look inside to start reading:

**https://mybook.to/BrightLiesPaperback**

ooo0ooo

AA Abbott has also written other psychological thrillers and the **Trail series** of thrillers, a lighter read sizzling with suspense and family drama. Take look at the first book in the series, **THE BRIDE'S TRAIL**. **Shady friends and sinister secrets. When a shy graduate finds herself framed, can she survive long enough to clear her name?**

**https://mybook.to/TheBridesTrailPback**

Visit AA Abbott's website to find out more, and sign up for her newsletter to receive a free ebook of short stories, news and offers.

**https://aaabbott.co.uk**

ooo0ooo

Did you enjoy **FLAT WHITE LIES?** Help other readers find their next psychological thriller – review this book on Amazon and Goodreads.

**Amazon: https://mybook.to/FlatWhiteLiesPaperback**

**Goodreads:**
**https://www.goodreads.com/book/show/196525118-flat-white-lies**
ooo0ooo

## ABOUT THE AUTHOR

British author AA Abbott, also known as Helen, writes suspense thrillers about women who find strength when they're facing deadly danger. Like Jenna Wyatt, she lives in a 19ᵗʰ century house in Bristol. She's also lived and worked in London and Birmingham, so all three cities feature in her intelligent and pacy novels.

While Helen is not dyslexic, many of her family are, which is why she is especially keen to make her books accessible. All of them are available in dyslexia-friendly large print as well as standard ebook and paperback editions. BRIGHT LIES is also available as an audiobook, recorded by award-winning voice actor Eilidh Beaton.

Find out more on Helen's website **https://aaabbott.co.uk/,**
Facebook **https://www.facebook.com/AAAbbottStories/,**
Instagram **https://www.instagram.com/aaabbottstories/,**
Threads **https://www.threads.net/@aaabbottstories,**
and Twitter **https://www.twitter.com/AAAbbottStories.**

ooo0ooo

## BOOKS BY A.A. ABBOTT

*Up In Smoke*

*After The Interview*

*The Bride's Trail*

*The Vodka Trail*

*The Grass Trail*

*The Revenge Trail*

*The Final Trail*

*Bright Lies*

*Lies at Her Door*

*Flat White Lies*

All books are available in ebook, standard paperback and large print (super-easy to read). FLAT WHITE LIES and other books are also available in hardback and BRIGHT LIES is available in audiobook.

oooOooo

## ABOUT BRIGHT LIES, AA ABBOTT'S DARKEST THRILLER

**He stole her childhood. Can she escape before he takes her life?**

Emily longs to be an artist. Her dream comes true when her new stepfather, a rich painter, begins mentoring her. But she's shocked to discover his dark side, and fear sends her fleeing his fancy home.

After facing further danger in a night on the streets, Emily accepts shelter in a squat. Building a future as an artist, she's terrified to learn her stepfather has turned to the media to hunt her down. Can she survive betrayal by her new friends and escape a killer's revenge?

If you enjoy nail-biting suspense, slow-burning secrets and dark domestic noir, you'll love AA Abbott's chilling psychological thriller.

**Read BRIGHT LIES today and stay by Emily's side as she runs for her life!**

**https://mybook.to/BrightLiesPaperback**

ooo0ooo

Printed in Great Britain
by Amazon

26499254R00098